Donald MacKenzie and The Murder Room

>>> This title is part of The Murder Room, our series dedicated to making available out-of-print or hard-to-find titles by classic crime writers.

Crime fiction has always held up a mirror to society. The Victorians were fascinated by sensational murder and the emerging science of detection; now we are obsessed with the forensic detail of violent death. And no other genre has so captivated and enthralled readers.

Vast troves of classic crime writing have for a long time been unavailable to all but the most dedicated frequenters of second-hand bookshops. The advent of digital publishing means that we are now able to bring you the backlists of a huge range of titles by classic and contemporary crime writers, some of which have been out of print for decades.

From the genteel amateur private eyes of the Golden Age and the femmes fatales of pulp fiction, to the morally ambiguous hard-boiled detectives of mid twentieth-century America and their descendants who walk our twenty-first century streets, The Murder Room has it all. >>>

The Murder Room
Where Criminal Minds Meet

themurderroom.com

T0352441

Donald MacKenzie 1908–1994

Donald MacKenzie was born in Ontario, Canada, and educated in England, Canada and Switzerland. For twenty-five years MacKenzie lived by crime in many countries. 'I went to jail,' he wrote, 'if not with depressing regularity, too often for my liking.' His last sentences were five years in the United States and three years in England, running consecutively. He began writing and selling stories when in American jail. 'I try to do exactly as I like as often as possible and I don't think I'm either psychopathic, a wayward boy, a problem of our time, a charming rogue. Or ever was.'

He had a wife, Estrela, and a daughter, and they divided their time between England, Portugal, Spain and Austria.

By Donald MacKenzie

Loose Cannon

Donald MacKenzie

An Orion book

Copyright © The Estate of Donald MacKenzie 1991

The right of Donald MacKenzie to be identified as the author of this work has been asserted in accordance with the Copyright, Designs and Patents Act 1988.

This edition published by
The Orion Publishing Group Ltd
Orion House
5 Upper St Martin's Lane
London WC2H 9EA

An Hachette UK company
A CIP catalogue record for this book is available from the British Library

ISBN 978 1 4719 0557 5

www.orionbooks.co.uk

Chapter One

An overhead sign flashed. FASTEN SEATBELTS! REFRAIN FROM SMOKING!

Philip Page reached for the buckle. The 747 tilted into the descent to Heathrow, offering a foreshortened view of bare trees and a chilly reservoir. It was almost noon. The Pan Am flight had left LA the previous evening and was arriving on schedule. The trim blonde hostess showed no sign of fatigue as she passed down the aisle, checking her charges. Page turned away, aware of his wrinkled tan suit and stubbled face.

It was almost twenty-four hours since the dusty Cadillac had roared up Carmel Valley and turned on to the road to Twin Oaks, scattering the horses behind the white-railed paddocks. After a brief conversation in the ranch-house, the two FBI agents had arrested Page on an extradition warrant and rushed him into federal court. Four hours later he was on his way to the airport, handcuffed to a taciturn Bostonian who spent most of the flight reading Longfellow.

The undercarriage thudded down. Page closed his eyes. He was forty-seven years old, of medium build, with rust-coloured hair and a belligerent stare. Three years living in California sunshine had turned his skin dark brown. His profile was blurred from too much Scotch. Wheels hit the tarmac in a three-point landing. Page kept his eyes shut. It had all happened too fast.

Ten a.m. on a perfect Pacific coast morning. He had been

1

walking the dogs along Pebble Beach. At a quarter past one on the same afternoon he was in federal court.

Slush fanned over Page's window. He opened his eyes. A hostess's voice sounded over the intercom. 'Please remain seated until the aircraft has come to a complete halt!'

The FBI agent removed his spectacles, put the volume of poems in his case and snapped a pair of plastic handcuffs on Page's wrists. The agent kept a firm grip on the unattached part of the links. Lights were burning throughout the airport buildings. A Pan Am jeep scooted across the wet tarmac, heading for the incoming plane. The aircraft stopped in front of the cocoon outside Terminal Two. Passengers left their seats, stretching and yawning, seeking their hand baggage in the overhead racks.

The agent came to his feet, bringing Page with him. He had used a razor while his prisoner dozed. Other passengers stood to one side as Page was led to the front of the aircraft. He was to be the first off the plane. Someone dropped the curtain in front of the first-class section. The bulkhead door was already open. A man from Pan Am ground staff stood with a clipboard, two plain-clothes policemen next to him.

The FBI agent nodded at the air hostess. 'Thanks for your help. I'll catch you another time!'

The shorter of the two waiting detectives made himself known. 'Agent Munro? I'm Detective Superintendent Manning, Fraud Squad. And this is Detective Sergeant Capstick.' The three men shook hands. Surrounding their charge, they negotiated a succession of corridors, passing through immigration and customs control to an empty office. Manning closed the door. 'You can take the cuffs off him now.'

Page stood still as the agent used the key. Manning and Agent Munro exchanged signatures on a couple of forms. Manning smiled. He had the enthusiastic manner of a scoutmaster, curly brown hair and distrustful eyes. Page took an instant dislike to him.

'Are you fixed up for a hotel?' Manning asked the agent. 'We didn't know what to do.'

The agent shook his head, looking at Page. 'I'm taking the plane back in the morning. You want to watch this character. He's got all the moves.' He lifted a hand and was gone.

Manning's expression changed as soon as the American left the room. 'Give you a hard time over there, did they?'

Page lit a Lucky. It was the first time he had been in police custody, but he had seen the films and TV. These clowns travelled in pairs, one kicking your ass while the other hung on to your hand. He made no reply to the question.

An unmarked police car was waiting in front of the building, a plain-clothes man at the wheel. Page sat in the back, flanked by the two detectives. Sleet obscured his view through the windows.

It was three years and two months since Page had left the UK, a few hours before the arrival of the Fraud Squad at his home in Chesham Street. Page's daughter had been in her last term at Saint Mary's, Ascot. The Pages did little entertaining. Page travelled a lot. His wife thought nothing of his absence until the Fraud Squad officers rang her doorbell. It was eighteen months after that when Page read of his wife's suicide. She had compounded a lethal concoction of whisky and seasickness pills and was found dead on the floor of the flat overlooking the river.

The car stopped in front of Chelsea police station. Page climbed the steps with his escort. A faint smell of disinfectant hung in the hallway. Typewriters clattered somewhere out of sight. A chest-high counter split the charge room in two. The desk sergeant looked up wearily. His tunic had grown too tight for him. Chrome numerals glittered on his shoulders. He leaned on his elbows and considered the three new arrivals.

'Philip Page, Sarge,' Manning said, jerking a thumb. 'Come all the way from California to see you.'

The sergeant spread himself comfortably, seized a form and glanced up at Page.

DONALD MACKENZIE

'Name?'

'Philip Page.'

'Date and place of birth?'

'April seventh, nineteen forty-three. Birthplace, Bruton, in Somerset.'

'Address?'

'Twin Oaks, Carmel, California.'

The sergeant closed his eyes briefly. 'Your address in this country.'

'I don't have one.' The admission prompted the question, 'When can I see a lawyer?'

'Later,' the sergeant replied automatically. 'Empty your pockets on to the counter. Your watch, too.'

The sergeant handled each article, describing it as he wrote in the property book. 'Six hundred and seven American dollars. One bunch of keys. One yellow metal Cartier watch, one yellow metal Dupont lighter. One Amex charge card.' He pushed the packet of Lucky Strike back across the counter. 'Let's have your belt.'

Page stared down at his midriff.

'I don't believe this,' he said, shaking his head.

The sergeant locked the property bag in a drawer. 'You're entitled to make one phone call to a solicitor of your choosing. If you want a member of your family to be informed, we'll take care of it.'

Page gave the number of Ruthrauf and Ryan, a firm of solicitors.

The sergeant handed Manning a bunch of cell keys. 'You lock him up, sir. Your legs are younger than mine.'

Manning accompanied Page down a flight of stone steps and unlocked a cell. The door closed, leaving Page alone. The cell was fifteen feet by eight with windows set high out of reach in the end wall. The sloping sill offered no purchase to a would-be climber. A coverless water closet dripped in a corner. A plank bed was cemented to the floor. There were no blankets or sheets. The door had been recently painted.

4

The scars of previous occupants' thinking still showed through new paint.

IF YOU LOVE IT SET IT FREE! IF IT DOESN'T COME BACK HUNT IT DOWN AND KILL IT!

The sentiment was close to Page's heart. Two names occupied his thoughts constantly. One of them was the witness who had made the statement that had brought Page back to England. He was not sure which of the two was the culprit.

Footsteps descended the steps outside. The hatch in the cell door was lowered. The hatless head of a uniformed policeman appeared.

'Come and get it!'

He pushed a paper bag and a mug of tea through the aperture. The hatch was lowered again.

Page carried the mug to the bench. The greasy paper bag contained a limp fried-egg sandwich. He pushed the food to one side and tasted the tea. It was stewed, hot and sweet and tasted like nectar. He finished it gratefully and rang the bell at the side of the door. The summons echoed along the corridor. It took three more rings to achieve a result. The cop reappeared, glaring indignantly through the open hatch.

'What do you want?'

Page held up the mug, smiling, his free hand supporting his trousers. 'Could I get some more of this?'

The cop's eyes rolled dangerously. 'Where the fuck do you think you are?' he snarled. 'The Ritz Hotel?' The hatch clattered down.

Time passed. Page had no watch but the light was fading outside. A hundred-watt bulb came on in the ceiling. More footsteps outside. This time the cell door was fully opened.

'Your brief's here,' said the cop.

The interview room was across the hall from the charge room. The cop let Page in and half closed the door. The man waiting inside was short and in his late forties. He was wearing a dark coat with a velvet collar and had gig-lamp spectacles. A briefcase was on the table in front of him.

'I'm Brian Loeb. We handle Ruthrauf and Ryan's criminal work. Take a seat.'

The two men sat down, facing one another across the bare deal table. The top of a baking-powder tin served as an ashtray.

Loeb produced a box of Balkan Sobranie. 'Smoke?'

Page shook his head, taking a Lucky Strike from his pocket. He used the lawyer's matches. 'They took my lighter away and – would you believe – my belt!'

The lawyer unscrewed a fountain pen and found a note-book. 'I've just had a word with the officer in charge of your case. Detective Superintendent Manning. He says you refused to make a statement. Is that correct?'

Page leaned back comfortably. 'Nobody ever got into trouble by keeping his mouth shut. I read that somewhere. What about bail?'

The lawyer blinked. 'There are a couple of things to get out of the way first. Ruthrauf and Ryan told me I had to look to you for funds.'

'So?'

Loeb took the question of money seriously. 'I've already talked to Matthew Horobin's clerk. Horobin's willing to take the brief. It's going to be an expensive business.'

'Lawyers generally are,' answered Page. 'Who is this guy?'

'Horobin.' Loeb repeated the name as if doing so increased his professional stature. 'He's a QC, the best fraud man in the country. But he's expensive. Fifteen hundred a day, five hundred for his junior and then, of course, there are my own fees. You're looking at the best part of three thousand pounds a day.'

Page lifted a shoulder. 'I'll deal with it just as soon as I can get to a phone. In the mean time you'd better take the name of a friend of mine. He'll supply whatever you need.'

The lawyer opened his notebook again. Page gave him a telephone number.

'His name's Henry Vyner. You'll get him at home in the evening. Tell him I'm going to need bail.'

'The police are bound to oppose,' said Loeb.

Page looked at him with sudden suspicion. 'How do you mean, oppose? I thought everyone was entitled to bail?'

'It doesn't work like that,' said the lawyer. The backs of his fingers grew fine black hair. There was more of the same in his ears that he picked under stress. 'An accused person is entitled to bail in theory but not if there are substantial grounds for believing that he may not turn up for his trial. Then there's the possibility of him interfering with witnesses.' He covered himself quickly. 'That's not me talking. It's what the police might say.'

It was thin ice they were skating on and Page wanted no part of it. 'If you're talking about this last piece of bullshit testimony, the name of the person who made the statement was never mentioned. How am I supposed to interfere with the Invisible Man?'

'Don't worry about it,' Loeb said quickly. 'Horobin'll take care of everything. If the magistrate refuses the bail application, we'll go to a judge in chambers.'

'You can explain all that to Henry Vyner,' said Page. 'He's a very rich man and an old friend of mine.'

Loeb looked at his watch and gathered his briefcase.

'I'd better get moving,' he said, standing up. 'I know it's a silly thing to say, but try to get some rest. Horobin and I will see you in court in the morning.'

He bustled through the door. The cop outside crooked a finger at Page and escorted him back to his cell.

Page was alone again, heartened by the lawyer's visit. Loeb was very different from the Ruthrauf and Ryan image of the corporate lawyers, equally at home in Canberra or Ottawa as in London. Loeb represented a direct line to QCs and judges in chambers.

The lamp burned all night in the ceiling. Page did his best to sleep, achieving no more than one catnap after another. He came alive with a start, conscious of someone standing in the open doorway.

'Rise and shine!' the cop said. 'Time to make yourself pretty for the magistrate.'

Page followed him to a tiled recess halfway along the corridor. An unframed mirror was stuck on the wall over a handbasin. There was soap, a towel and a safety razor. Page scraped his face smooth and combed his hair. His lightweight tan suit had been slept in for two nights in succession, and looked like it. What Page saw in the mirror did nothing to reassure him.

His next stop was the charge room. The desk sergeant returned Page's property. Page buckled on his belt and pocketed his belongings.

'What about my passport?' he asked.

The desk sergeant wheezed and smiled. 'Thinking of going somewhere, were you? See Superintendent Manning. I'm sure he'll be glad to accommodate you.'

Page sat on a bench in the charge room. Half an hour passed. The door to the yard was opened. Cold air blew in, bringing a flurry of snowflakes with it. A couple of uniformed cops bustled in wearing greatcoats. They were part of the crew of the Black Maria waiting in the yard outside.

'I got a live one for you gents this morning,' the desk sergeant said, leaning his belly against the edge of the counter. He nodded across at Page.

The escort took the typewritten sheet that accompanied Page and jerked his head. The back of the Black Maria was open. There were five cubicles on each side of the vehicle. Page was locked in one of them. Doors slammed. The escort climbed into the cab with the driver. The Black Maria lumbered out of the yard into the street. Page was standing up, his head twisted so that he had a foreshortened view of what was happening outside. The street-lamps still burned although it was nine fifteen. Swirling snow cut visibility to a few yards. Lines of glum-faced passengers waited at bus stops, heads wrapped in hats and scarves.

Horseferry Road Magistrates' Court was the first stop. Page and a Jamaican wearing a multi-coloured woollen cap were ushered into a brightly lit corridor and handed over to a waiting sergeant with a clipboard. A door closed on the Jamaican. Another lock turned on Page. The cell was smaller than the one he had previously occupied. There was the same plank bed, water closet and high, barred window. He had three cigarettes left. He lit one with the matches he had filched from the lawyer. It was a quarter past ten by his watch when the cell door reopened. The cop with the clipboard looked in.

'Philip Page?'

'That's me.' Page came to his feet.

The jailer sprang the tongue of the lock, ensuring that it could not be closed accidentally.

'Some people to see you,' he said. He moved to one side, allowing Loeb and an older man to enter the cell. The door was partially closed. Loeb's black wiry hair had been carefully groomed. He wore a dark business suit and carried his briefcase.

'This is Matthew Horobin, your barrister,' he said, making the introduction. 'There are a couple of things to discuss before going into court.'

The QC was a strong-featured man in his mid-fifties, wearing a double-breasted navy blue suit with a rosebud in his lapel. His inspection of Page was thorough.

'How are you?' he asked, pushing his hand out.

'I've been a lot better,' Page admitted. His first impression of Horobin was a good one. The barrister's grave manner was reassuring. It was like having a judge in your corner. A man like this conversed with the establishment on equal terms. Loeb took a seat on the end of the plank bed, his briefcase in his lap, for the moment to withdraw from the conversation. Horobin glanced round the cell and frowned. 'I imagine this is the first time you've been in a place like this.'

'That's right,' said Page, 'and I don't much like it.'

'Nobody does,' Horobin said. 'That's why we've got to get you out of here quickly, on bail. I've been through all the material Mr Loeb was able to find. Newspaper reports and so on. None of it's evidential, of course, but it does help to provide a background.'

Page extinguished his cigarette. Headlines revived in his memory.

FRAUD SQUAD OFFICERS VISIT BELGRAVIA HOME
MISSING ENTREPRENEUR SOUGHT IN CITY SCANDAL

'What you've read was based upon hearsay and lies,' he said. 'The only facts were the names of the people concerned. What you don't seem to understand is that I'm innocent!' He realised that he had raised his voice and forced himself to speak quietly. 'The British government tried to get me extradited on two occasions. Both times they failed. So they tried again. This time they succeeded. The fact remains that I'm innocent.'

The QC moved his head in sympathy. 'Neither Mr Loeb nor I would be representing you otherwise.'

Page disbelieved the statement entirely.

Leob looked up. 'In any case, it isn't us that you have to convince – it's the jury.'

Horobin shifted from one leg to another. The closeness of the cell seemed to affect him.

'The first objective is to get you out on bail. The police will do their best to oppose it. Miss Lassiter is representing the DPP. The reasons she'll produce are the obvious ones. The amount of money involved. The fact that you left the country without telling anyone – including your family, as I understand it. Then there are the old stand-bys. They'll claim that you won't respond to your bail if it's granted, interfere with witnesses.'

Page was outraged. 'You mean they can say stuff like that and get away with it?'

'I'm afraid so,' said Horobin.

'I don't believe this!' Page said heatedly. 'I left this country openly on a ticket that had my name on it. I hadn't even been questioned by the police at that stage and I used my own passport. What was I supposed to do – put an advertisement in *The Times*?'

Horobin looked at the end of his cigarette. 'The prosecution will say that the police had no opportunity to question you, you weren't there. We've got one thing in our favour. We're up in front of Hugh Graham. He's got a mind of his own and he listens to both sides. He rarely gets a reversal. Apart from the bail application, your appearance here this morning is no more than a formality.'

The corridor outside was rowdy. Doors were being opened and shut, names being called. The jailer poked his head into the cell.

'Court's in session, gents. You've got another fifteen minutes.' The three men checked their watches.

Loeb resumed the conversation. 'This statement they referred to in the federal court. Did you ever see it?'

'I neither saw nor heard it,' said Page. 'The lawyer for the British government referred to fresh evidence, but they never produced it. Nor was the name of the witness ever mentioned.'

'We'll know soon enough,' said Horobin. 'They'll have to provide us with copies of any documentary evidence they're going to use before the trial. Leave everything to me once we're in court. All you have to do is answer to your name.'

The entrance to the courtroom was no more than ten feet away. The door was thrown open. The Jamaican in the Rastafarian colours emerged shouting abuse. Page took his place in the dock. There was room enough for half a dozen prisoners, a bench to sit on and a ledge on which to write. The magistrate sat on a red upholstered chair under the royal arms. There were four rows of benches between the magistrate and the dock. The clerk of the court and stenographer sat next to one another. Horobin and the woman barrister occupied the front row, Loeb and a man from the treasury solicitor's department behind them. The public and press galleries were full. The sergeant with the clipboard stood at the side of the dock.

The court clerk rose, reading from the paper he was holding. 'Is your full name Philip Page?'

The jailer urged Page to stand. 'Yes, it is,' Page replied.

'Philip Page, you are charged on two counts under the Fraud Act of 1982. Do you plead guilty or not guilty?'

Horobin rose, clutching his lapels with both hands. 'I appear for the defendant, Your Honour. The defendant pleads not guilty to both charges.'

The woman barrister rose in turn. 'I appear for the Crown, Your Honour.'

'Thank you, Miss Lassiter. You may call your first witness.'

There was general shuffling of feet. Detective Superintendent Manning crossed the courtroom to the witness box. Page turned his head towards the public gallery. His daughter was sitting in the second row next to Henry Vyner. It was more than three years since Page had seen either of them. Vyner lifted a hand in salute.

The detective superintendent took the oath. Miss Lassiter began her examination.

'Please give your full name and rank.'

'William Makepeace Manning. Detective superintendent attached to the Fraud Squad.' He spread his legs and assumed the at-ease position.

The barrister glanced up at the magistrate. 'May the officer refer to his notes, Your Honour?'

The dialogue was stylised, question and answer known in advance.

'How long after the events were the notes made?' asked the magistrate.

'Twenty minutes, Your Honour.'

The magistrate looked down at Horobin. 'Any objections, Mr Horobin?'

Horobin shook his head. 'None, Your Honour.'

The questioning continued. 'Officer, did you take the defendant into custody yesterday at Heathrow Airport?'

'I did, madam. I told him who I was and that I would be charging him with two offences under the Fraud Act of 1982. I also said that I would be taking him to Chelsea police station where he would be charged and kept in custody until his appearance before a magistrates' court. I informed him that he was not obliged to say anything. but that anything he did say might be used in evidence.'

Page turned his head again, unable to resist the temptation to look at the public benches. The last few years had draped Vyner's frame with still more flesh. Page's daughter refused to look at him.

Miss Lassiter continued. 'What happened next?'

'The defendant was conveyed to Chelsea police station, Your Honour. He was charged and informed of his rights again. He declined to make a statement and asked to see a lawyer.'

'And was that request complied with?'

'Yes it was, madam. Contact was made with a firm of solicitors. One of their representatives is in court now.' He looked directly at Loeb.

The magistrate shifted in his seat. 'Any questions for this witness, Mr Horobin?'

'None, Your Honour.'

Manning left the witness box and seated himself near the dock. Miss Lassiter resumed her role.

'This is a complex case, Your Honour, involving a number

of enquiries being made in several countries. Witnesses have to be contacted. Statements have to be taken. The prosecution is requesting a two-week remand.'

The magistrate and his clerk conferred. The magistrate looked down at the lawyers.

'How about the fourteenth of November?'

Miss Lassiter smiled. 'Fine, for my part, Your Honour. The prosecution should be in a position to proceed at that time.'

The magistrate cocked his head. 'Mr Horobin?'

'It suits me, Your Honour. The question of bail remains. The defendant has been extradited from the United States of America on charges of fraud. These charges will be vigorously refuted, Your Honour. It will be impossible to prepare a proper defence if the defendant is kept in custody. The police are already in possession of his passport and he is prepared to report to them daily. A friend of the defendant is in court, Your Honour. He is ready to enter into whatever recognisances Your Honour may require.'

It was the woman lawyer's turn again, calm and quite sure of herself.

'My instructions are that the police strongly object to bail being granted, Your Honour. The defendant fled the country more than three years ago. He was ultimately traced to California. The police feel that he would abscond if granted bail. There's the additional problem of witnesses being tampered with.'

Horobin rose with authority. His voice was heavy with indignation.

'With great respect, Your Honour, this is clearly a case in which bail should be granted. My client is a man of unblemished character with a complete answer to the charges that have been brought against him. Miss Lassiter has referred to "fleeing the country". My client did no such thing. He left quite openly. No one attempted to detain or question him at that time. This case is likely to drag on into March, even later.

To keep an innocent man in custody for that length of time is, in my submission, intolerable.'

She was back like a terrier. 'The defendant has no fixed abode in this country.'

Horobin adjusted his spectacles and looked at her. 'That has been taken care of, Your Honour. A flat in London has been put at my client's disposal. The police are aware of this and should Your Honour be disposed to grant bail, the police are satisfied with the surety.'

The magistrate and his clerk went into a huddled conference. The magistrate came out of it, looking down at the lawyers before him.

'I have decided to allow bail in this instance. There will be one surety in the amount of five hundred thousand pounds, subject to the following conditions. The defendant will be required to report daily to the local police station between the hours of five and eight p.m.'

Detective Superintendent Manning swivelled in his seat, a hand over his mouth guiding his voice towards the sergeant behind. Page was close enough to hear what he said. 'That's the last we'll see of him.'

Horobin shook Page by the hand. 'Either Mr Loeb or I will be in contact. If you have any problem at all, get in touch with him.' He wagged a finger. 'And stay away from the press!'

The courtroom was emptying. A new audience surged in. Loeb accompanied Page to the lifts. Henry Vyner fell in step beside Page. Once in the lift, Vyner and Page looked at one another.

'It's been a long time,' Vyner said quietly. He was a large and heavy man with an almost bald head and pendulous cheeks. He was the same age as Page but looked ten years older. Expensive tailoring failed to conceal the excess weight he was carrying.

'A long time, Henry,' Page echoed.

The bail office was on the second floor. The cage began its ascent. After the first greeting, Page kept his eyes on the ground. For more than three years he had dreaded meeting his daughter. He had been accused of deserting both her and her mother. Marian's suicide had only increased the volume of stricture. Not one of the accusations was true. The Department of Trade and Industry was already investigating his affairs at the time he left England. Any money transferred to his wife risked confiscation. Henry Vyner had come up with the solution. Page had paid a million pounds into an account with Privatbank in Zürich. A trust was administered by Vyner in favour of Page's wife and daughter. It was additional proof of Vyner's unassailable loyalty.

The lift stopped and the doors slid open.

Drusilla Page was waiting outside the bail office. She was bundled into a green loden coat and had straight shoulder-length hair a shade or two lighter than her father's. Her green eyes considered him from a face wiped clear of all expression. She was wearing no make-up except for gloss on her lips.

Page lifted her chin with his hand. 'Hi, darling!' he said, softly.

She looked past him at Vyner. 'Do you mind if my father and I have a few words in private, Uncle Henry?'

'Go ahead,' Vyner said. He pushed the door of the bail office and went inside. Loeb went with him.

Drusilla spoke very quietly. 'Me being here is Uncle Henry's idea. I didn't want to come. What you did to Mamma was unforgivable. She always defended you, and I believed her. But not any more. I blame you for her death.'

He felt the blood surge in his face and neck and tried to control his temper. 'Have you finished?' he asked.

Her voice was barely audible. 'I despise you.'

He could see Vyner and Superintendent Manning inside the bail office, chatting away like old friends. He pushed his shaking hands deep in his pockets.

'Then what are you doing here?'

Her mouth trembled. She was close to tears. 'You wouldn't understand,' she said bitterly. 'It's too late in any case.

Mamma's dead and you're going to prison. I don't want to have you on my conscience.'

'I don't believe this!' he said despairingly. 'You're my daughter, for God's sake!'

Her smile was completely joyless. 'I was your daughter three years ago. It didn't stop you walking out on us. Mamma would still be alive if it hadn't been for you.'

Loeb pushed the door open. If he was aware of the tension he showed no sign of it.

'All we need is a couple of signatures and you're a free man,' he said cheerfully.

The clerk dealing with the bail application was talking to Superintendent Manning. He slid two forms in front of Page and pointed. 'If you'll sign here, please.' The clerk was clearly impressed by the size of the money involved.

Manning still made his presence felt. 'About the reporting,' he said to Page. 'That's done daily between the hours of five and eight p.m. at Chelsea police station. If you're sick, you'll need a doctor's certificate. If you want to leave the country, an application will have to be made to the court.'

'How would I do that?' asked Page. 'You've got my passport.'

He continued to look at the superintendent. Of all those supposed to be in his corner, Vyner was the only one he was sure of.

Loeb made his excuses, leaving his home number with Page. Drusilla was waiting by the lift when Page caught up with her.

'We've got to talk,' he said, quietly.

Drusilla averted her face.

His memory was swift and sad. Her first term at Saint Mary's. He was dropping her off at the school. They had been close in those days, sure of one another's love and loyalty. He had delivered her to the sister in charge of new girls. He remembered the desperation with which his daughter had clung to him.

'Do whatever you think is right,' he had said. 'And try not to hurt other people.'

He caught her arm again and the lift doors opened.

'We've got to talk,' he repeated.

She broke free, moving her head from side to side.

'You and I have nothing to say to one another. Talk to Uncle Henry if you need someone to talk to. He's the best friend you've got, the only one probably.'

He watched as she ran for a taxi in the snow. Vyner had gone to the Cadogan Hotel. Page waited until another cab emptied outside. He climbed into the back with a feeling of total loneliness.

Vyner was overflowing a chair in the lobby. He rose nimbly for a man of his size. Three strides brought him to Page. He looked at Page closely.

'How did it go?' he asked anxiously.

The foyer was crowded with expensive voices and clothes, all vying for attention. It reminded Page of his own dishevelled appearance. He waited until they were seated at table before answering Vyner's question.

'My daughter hates me,' Page said dejectedly. 'It's as simple as that. Can you imagine, Henry? She accused me of some pretty unpleasant things. She blames me for Marian's death and says that I deserted them. If it hadn't been for you, and so on.'

Vyner picked at the inside of a bread roll. 'I did exactly what you told me to do,' he said. 'Neither Marian nor Drusilla knew where the money came from. Nobody knew except you, me and Herr Vogel at Privatbank. Dolphin Square was bought in Marian's name. She left it to Drusilla. They both thought that I provided the money. Drusilla still thinks so.'

'It was your idea in the first place,' said Page. 'And of course you were right. The Department of Trade and Industry would have grabbed every penny otherwise. Just the same, it's an ugly way to lose a daughter.'

'Don't be ridiculous,' Vyner replied. 'All it needs is a

little time. Drusilla's been through a lot in the last couple of years.'

Page tasted the sorrel soup without relish. He knew nothing about his daughter's activities since he had left England. There had been no correspondence between them. The two men ate their way through poached turbot served with an anchovy sauce and new potatoes. It was very different to the Carmel Cookhouse.

Page spoke through his last mouthful. 'Has Drusilla got a boyfriend?'

'Not one that she talks about, anyway. She spends a lot of time with a girl she works with at Christie's. Don't get me wrong,' he said hurriedly. 'It's just a phase that she's going through. In any case, she's not twenty-one yet.'

Page's mind was still restless. 'You're sure Drusilla has no idea that the money for the trust came from me?'

'Positive,' replied Vyner. 'I got the Privatbank lawyers to set up the trust. Marian and Drusilla were joint beneficiaries after Dolphin Square was bought. Drusilla gets the income until she's thirty or marries, then the capital. She calls it the "Uncle Henry Trust".' His smile was embarrassed. 'I'm sorry about that.'

'You've got no cause to apologise,' Page said quickly. 'You did everything that I asked you to do and I'm grateful.' He finished the last of the wine in his glass. 'How about you, Henry? Do you hold me responsible for Marian's death?'

It was an ugly question, whatever the answer.

'We've got to have a proper light on this,' Page went on.

Vyner brooded for a while then looked up sadly. 'I was too shocked to blame anyone. I'd seen Marian that afternoon for tea. She went home and swallowed twenty Magamine tablets and a half-bottle of Scotch. She had nothing left to live for. It was as simple as that.'

Page wiped his mouth with his napkin. 'That's not a proper answer. I asked if you held me responsible.'

Vyner moved his head in negation. 'Your marriage was

finished the moment you had Drusilla. You had your child and as far as you were concerned, that was the end of it. Marian was no more than an ornament from that moment on. She resented it.'

'Did she leave any message?'

'Nothing,' said Vyner. 'She'd made her will six months before. Everything went to Drusilla except that little gold lion you gave her.'

'What happened to that?'

'She left it to me,' Vyner said quietly. He called for the bill.

A waiter brought it with the news that Vyner's car was outside. A dark-blue Bentley Continental was drawn up in front of the Sloane Street entrance. A Filipino dressed in chauffeur's livery sat behind the wheel. Page smiled to himself. Vyner had always been grand, even at prep school. They drove south to the Embankment and stopped outside some houses that faced the river.

Vyner leaned forward and spoke to the driver. 'Wait here for me.'

Page followed him out on to the pavement. Vyner looked up at the elegant red-brick façade.

'This is it. There are only three other people living in the house. The housekeeper – she's in the basement – and a South African couple. They're away for the winter. You're at the top.'

Vyner opened a comfortably furnished hallway with bronze chrysanthemums glowing on a side table. The lift rose silently and stopped at the penthouse. Vyner selected two more keys and stood to one side, allowing Page to enter the flat first. The cream-painted hallway was bright with more flowers and brightly polished silver. Vyner collected a couple of letters from a tray.

'I slept here last night as soon as I had your news. I hadn't been up for a couple of weeks.'

He led the way into a sitting room with a high Edwardian

ceiling and large windows overlooking the Embankment and the river. It was almost half past three and the light was fading fast. Vyner touched a switch, filling the room with soft light.

'You'll be comfortable here. The housekeeper takes care of the cleaning and whatever shopping you need. She'll see that your laundry is done, as well. You'll find her discreet and honest.'

There were Persian rugs on the parquet floor, a matching pair of Louis Seize couches. A Stubbs horse painting hung on the wall. There were family photographs and a presentation plaque from Battersea Dogs' Home.

Vyner smiled. 'I keep forgetting – you've never been here before. Let's take a look at the rest of it.'

They made the tour, Vyner in front, opening doors. 'This is the kitchen. I never use it, but you'll find everything's there. And this is the bathroom.' There was a sunken tub with a mirror at chest level. The Royal Hospital gardens extended below. Pigeons perched on such elms as survived.

Vyner opened another door. 'Two bedrooms. I thought you'd prefer this one.' A cream-painted wardrobe covered one entire wall. Vyner slid a door back, revealing a row of vinyl-enclosed suits on hangers, shelves full of laundered shirts and socks, shoes in their trees.

Vyner held his rare smile. 'Everything you left behind at Chesham Street, Philip. Marian asked me to take care of it. It's all here, you'll find.'

'Good Lord,' Page said in wonder. The cane-headed bed had come from his bedroom at Chesham Street. 'Did Marian ever mention any papers to you?'

Vyner looked up from checking the heating control. 'Papers? What sort of papers?'

'Business,' Page said vaguely. 'Accounts, invoices, a desk diary, that sort of thing. Some stuff that I asked her to dispose of.'

Vyner shook his head. 'The only papers I saw were your

marriage certificate and a few odds and sods from Eton. Photographs and stuff. They're in the other room.'

They returned to the sitting room. Vyner opened a bureau. He displayed a small leather wallet. 'Your documents,' he said. He put the wallet back and gave Page an envelope. 'You may have some delay with bank transfers. There's five thousand pounds there. Let me know if you need any more.' He had the demeanour of a cardinal dispensing largesse. 'Everything except a woman,' he said. 'I thought you'd prefer to take care of that yourself.'

They were joking now and Page was glad of it. He felt in his pockets for cigarettes. The packet was empty.

'Cheroots,' said Vyner, pointing at a box on the table. 'No cigarettes, I'm afraid.'

Page clipped the end from a panatella. He carried it to one of the couches.

'We never had the same taste in women, come to think of it.' He blew smoke at the ceiling. 'Except for Marian, of course.'

'Except for Marian,' Vyner agreed. There was no jealousy in his tone, merely acceptance. It had been Vyner who introduced Page to Marian. Ten months later she married him.

Vyner sat down facing Page. 'Do you feel like talking or not?'

'About what?' Page cocked his head.

'What happened with you and Consol Electric.'

Page settled back on the cushions. 'I've already told you.'

Vyner frowned. 'They weren't exactly what I'd call comfortable conversations, Philip. You called me twice from California. All I knew then was what I read in the newspapers. I've never really heard your side of the story.'

'And that's what you want to hear?'

'I'm your friend,' Vyner said chidingly. 'At the moment it's like looking into a mirror that's covered with dust. I want to know what went wrong.'

Page stretched his legs. Apart from the lawyers, Vyner was the first to have asked for his side of the story.

'I can't remember where you were that summer,' he said.

'I went to Japan in May, got back in August. By then you were gone.'

Double glazing deadened the sound from outside. It was easy to recreate the memory.

'It started some time in April. I was still going to Crockford's. Somebody introduced me to a Pakistani called Rasheed Ferook. He was playing chemmy. I thought no more about it at the time. Then I ran into Ferook again at one of Luci Sale's parties. He turned out to be a colonel in the Pakistani Air Force, over here buying equipment.'

Vyner was listening, eyes half closed, his hands clasped on his bulging stomach.

'You can imagine,' said Page, 'as soon as I knew who he was I started making more enquiries. We went over to Deauville together for the weekend. By then we were friends. He told me about this deal he was setting up. The Pakistani Air Force needed gunsights. Ferook knew of this firm called Pantile HiTek. He said that these people had the workforce and expertise necessary. The contract would be worth eighteen million. Ferook figured that he and I could do business together. He said there'd be no problems with the Ministry of Defence.'

Vyner opened his eyes. 'So you bought Pantile HiTek?'

'That's right,' said Page. 'I borrowed three and a half million pounds from the bank. I had to put up everything I owned as security. The house in Chesham Street, insurance policies, the lot. I bought Pantile HiTek lock, stock and barrel. It was a small company, just a mother and two sons on the board. They were delighted. By this time Ferook was back in Pakistan, preparing the contracts. Have you any idea at all what goes on in that sort of world, Henry?'

'Not a thing,' Vyner admitted.

Page laughed. 'All I knew was what Ferook told me. I

learned quickly. It's a game that's played with some very weird rules. In the first place, no one admits to anything. There's that thing called "confidentiality". There are plenty of rumours. Who's doing what and so forth. But nobody's able to prove a thing until the deal is tied up. Anyway, by this time, Consol Electric had wind of the project. They had already done work for the Saudis. They wanted more of the same. Someone called my office and asked for a meeting, someone from Consol Electric. Two of them arrived, wearing big poker smiles. They banged on about the importance of centralisation. They wanted to buy Pantile HiTek, plus any existing contracts they had on their books. They offered me fourteen million.'

Vyner clucked. 'That sounds like asking for trouble on their part. You pay three and a half. They offer four times as much without sight of the contracts you're supposed to have.'

'*Had*,' emphasised Page. 'The contracts were about to be signed. I took Consol's offer. As you say, I'd quadrupled my money. All I did was apply prior knowledge. It's done every day in the City, Henry. Consol Electric were banking that the contracts existed.'

'But they didn't,' said Vyner.

'Maybe not physically,' argued Page. 'But as far as I was concerned, they were in preparation. I acted in total good faith. Then four days after we signed, Ferook was on the plane with President Zia. The CIA blew them out of the sky.'

Vyner looked as though he had just been insulted. 'The CIA?'

'Whoever,' Page said impatiently. 'The point is that Bhutto got herself elected and began to clean house. No one was left from Zia's regime. Even the girls on the switchboard were sacked. The only thing left of Ferook was his name on the passenger list. Of course Bhutto's gone now, too.'

Vyner seemed spellbound. 'I already knew a lot of this. The media made a meal of it.'

'They're full of shit,' said Page. 'I never had the chance to

fulfil the promises I made. OK, what do *you* think I should
have done?'

Vyner heaved himself up and went to the window. He stood
looking down at the street. He turned.

'I'm not the right person to ask.'

'Why not?' said Page. 'Everyone else is sticking in his two
cents' worth.'

'I'm not on the jury,' said Vyner.

Page hit himself hard on the forehead. 'Here we go again
with the jury! That's all I've been getting from the lawyers.'

Vyner returned to his seat. He lowered himself carefully
hitching up his trouser-legs.

'Morally you may have a case. It's the legal aspect we've
got to worry about.'

A thought set Page alight again. 'Are you saying that
morality's got nothing to do with justice, Henry?'

Vyner was silent.

'Come on, now,' Page insisted. 'Answer me.'

Vyner moved heavy shoulders. 'I talked to Horobin before
we went into court this morning. You know, about how he'd
get paid and so on. He says he's worried about this new
evidence, the statement that's been made.'

'Lies,' replied Page. 'Every word of it.'

'Whoever it is must have known what was happening,'
Vyner said gently.

'OK,' said Page. 'It's got to be one of two people. Marcus
Poole is one of them. He was Consol Electric's financial
adviser. He's the less likely of the two. He knew what
was going down. He bought Consol Electric shares on the
strength of it. That was insider dealing, a criminal offence
even then.'

Vyner lifted his massive head. 'And the other one?'

'Some lawyer I used called O'Callaghan. We used to have
a drink together in the evening. Even that doesn't seem right.
He knew that I was in the middle of an important deal, but
that's all. This statement's supposed to cite chapter and verse,

claiming that I knew that the contracts didn't exist when I signed with Consol Electric.'

The couch sagged as Vyner shifted his weight. 'Horobin said something about you having your desk diary shredded before the DTI inspectors had a chance to look at it.'

'More garbage,' Page said heatedly. 'I don't know where they get this stuff. There *was* no desk diary. Anyway, the DTI weren't involved at that stage.'

'But the damage was done,' replied Vyner. 'You'd left the country.'

'For crissakes,' Page said. 'Whose side are you supposed to be on? The Fraud Squad went to see Marcus Poole. He had the perfect answer. "Philip Page? I always assumed that he had the contracts tucked safely away. Given his reputation I had complete faith in him."'

Vyner was sitting upright again. His weight appeared to spread laterally. 'God knows I'm no lawyer, but it seems to me that everything's going to hang on the question of intent. I mean, your intent at the moment you accepted Consol Electric's cheque.'

'So we're back to the jury again,' countered Page. 'What are they, these jurymen – born again Christians? They're just twelve run-of-the-mill people, Henry. The less sophisticated they are, the more they believe in abstract concepts like honour and justice. It helps them to sleep at night. The corporate conscience, that's what they are. And that's where my problem lies.' He opened the box of panatellas and lit another. 'The Brits tried to extradite me on two occasions, right? They failed because of insufficient evidence. By then I'd bought the place in the Valley. I paid taxes, joined the country club and danced with Clint Eastwood's wife. People liked me, Henry. They came up and shook my hands after the first two hearings. The third time the Brits succeeded. I hadn't ripped off the widows and orphans, remember. I'd clobbered Consol Electric for fourteen million. That's worse than rape.'

Vyner glanced across the room. Snowflakes were sailing in front of the window panes.

'I'd better start making tracks,' he said, 'before the roads get really bad.'

Page accompanied him to the lift. Vyner pulled the gate open. The cage moved perceptibly under his weight. His face was grave. 'Don't worry about Drusilla,' he said.

Chapter Two

John Raven woke to the sound of the telephone ringing. He felt for the handset. It was suddenly quiet on the boat. Snowflakes fluttered across the gap in the curtains.

A man's voice sounded very close in Raven's ear. 'It's me. Patrick.'

Raven propped himself up on the pillows. 'Have you any idea what the time is?' The answer was on the face of the travelling clock by his bedside. It was nine fifteen on a winter morning with Kirstie six thousand miles away. Impossible to blame her for the disturbance.

'I know the time,' his friend said urgently. 'I've got to see you right away.'

Raven swallowed a yawn. 'Where are you?'

'I'm in a phone box at South Kensington underground station.' O'Callaghan sounded agitated.

'Then you'd better come round,' Raven said. Patrick O'Callaghan was friend and lawyer. Raven's first unlikely thought was of trouble between O'Callaghan and his wife. 'Bring the papers and the post in with you,' he said.

'I'll be there in fifteen minutes,' said the lawyer.

Raven swung his legs from the bed and stretched. He found his blue towelling bathrobe and opened the curtains. An east wind was blowing the snow up river. The stuff was an inch thick on the window ledge. It was difficult to make out the trees on the south side of the Thames. He went into the kitchen, switched on the overhead light and filled the coffee percolator. The tyre fenders groaned and creaked, the mooring-chains clanked. There was little noise up on the Embankment.

After eighteen years as a cop, Raven could jump in and out of his clothes as fast as a model. It took him seven minutes flat to shave, pull on a pair of jeans and a turtle-neck sweater. By this time the coffee was brewing. He carried the tray into the sitting room. This was forty feet by eighteen and covered more than half of the red-cedar superstructure. Panoramic double-glazed windows followed the line of the hull. An electric motor dragged brocade curtains along overhead rails. Once closed, the room was completely cut off from the outside world. There were two bedrooms, one on each side of the bathroom. A corridor ran lengthways from the sitting room to the bow of the boat. The kitchen was off the corridor.

The *Albatross* had been built for the grain trade, hauling barley from East Anglia to the breweries along the banks of the Thames. The original hull had been decked with timber cannibalised from other boats. The conversion left a large space below the kitchen. This was reached by a ladder and was used as a storeroom and cellar. Most of the furniture on the boat had come with Kirstie from Canada, Victorian reproductions of Hepplewhite chairs and tables. There was a large couch and a French desk. A much-darned Aubusson covered the floor. One wall was fronted by white-painted cupboards and shelves. There was a Bang & Olufsen Beocenter, two large speakers and storage space for records and tapes. A picture-light shone on Raven's prize possession, a study in blue and black by Paul Klee.

The boat was the only real home that Raven had ever had. For the last seven years he had shared it with his Canadian wife. Her photograph stood on the desk. The pose showed her shielding her eyes from the sun, her honey-blonde hair reaching down to her shoulders. Written underneath were the words: May the love last as long as the bone structure!

The door buzzer sounded. Raven pressed a button, releasing the door at the foot of the stone steps leading down from the Embankment. He moved to the window. Patrick O'Callaghan appeared, his feet in galoshes, tracking through the snow. Raven hurried his friend into the warmth of the sitting room, took the newspapers and post and helped the lawyer to take off his overcoat.

O'Callaghan sat down heavily on the chintz-covered couch. Raven considered him. 'You look like shit,' he said after a while. He put milk and sugar into the coffee cup and gave it to his friend.

O'Callaghan was a small neat man with lank mid-brown hair, a thin moustache and dark-blue eyes with large pupils. He was wearing a grey tweed suit with cuffs on the sleeves. His striped-silk bow tie was lopsided. Raven had never seen him looking so worried.

The lawyer tasted his coffee briefly and put the cup down again.

'You're not going to believe this,' he warned, wiping his moustache with his handkerchief.

'Believe what?' demanded Raven. He was usually good in the morning but with Kirstie in Canada he had taken to sleeping late.

O'Callaghan pulled a cassette from his jacket pocket. 'Just listen to this!' he said.

Raven looked at the tape. 'What the hell is it?'

'Play it,' the lawyer insisted. 'It's the tape from my answering machine.'

Raven dropped the tape into place on the Beocenter. He settled back on the couch next to his friend. A man's voice sounded, loud in the eighteen-inch speakers.

'You and I have to talk, O'Callaghan. You owe me that much at least.'

The tape clicked to a stop.

Raven grimaced. 'So what?'

The lawyer brushed away an invisible fly. 'I'm thankful that

30

Maureen didn't get to it first. She'd have freaked out. Does the name Philip Page mean anything to you?'

Raven nodded down at the newspaper on the the carpet. It was yesterday's *Mail*. A banner headline screamed across the front page. ABSCONDING FINANCIER ARRESTED AT HEATHROW.

'It was on the news last night,' he volunteered. 'The guy who took off with all that loot.'

'That's his voice you just heard,' the lawyer said solemnly. 'I can't afford to be involved in stuff like this. It would finish me. My career would be ruined.'

Raven grinned openly. 'You know what they say, no smoke without fire.'

The lawyer's mouth twitched. 'This isn't a joke. Page is out on bail and I'm in bad trouble.'

'Hold it a minute!' said Raven behind uplifted hands. He was six feet three inches tall with the rangy build of a basketball player. The hair that was mostly grey had once been blond. He looked at his friend, shaking his head slowly. This wasn't the man he knew, the suave advocate undisturbed by the grossest of truths. O'Callaghan had the mien of someone who has just found six ounces of Semtex under his mattress.

'What's the problem?' asked Raven. 'I get this kind of crap at least twice a month. People I put inside all those years ago. Hard-nosed coppers still on the job calling me renegade. You just have to learn to live with it.'

At any other time, Raven would have continued to reason with his friend. The expression on the lawyer's face warned against it.

'OK,' said Raven. 'Tell me about it.'

O'Callaghan stroked his chin. Then he shook his head again. 'This goes back more than three years, John. Someone sent Page to the office. He wanted me to handle his personal business. You know, the sort of thing I do for you and Kirstie. He seemed a nice enough chap on the surface. Interesting,

31

in fact, at the beginning. And he paid his bills promptly. I liked him. Then he started coming round to the office late in the afternoon. We'd go out for a drink together. What he really needed was an audience. He said he never discussed business at home and he needed to talk. This was about the time when he was doing business with Consol Electric. He told me he owned this electronic company outside Reading. He was doing some deal with the Pakistanis. Are you listening to what I'm saying?'

'Every word,' Raven said hastily.

O'Callaghan grunted. 'Page never went into details. Nor did I ask. As I said, all he needed was someone to talk to.' The lawyer's voice dropped. 'Then one night I saw his violent side. We were in a cab going somewhere or other. He accused the driver of taking us out of our way. I didn't realise how drunk Page was. The driver was indignant. Page continued to be abusive. The driver locked both doors. Next thing I knew we were in the police station. It took a lot of talking before they let us go.'

'That's what alcohol does for you,' Raven said, glancing across at the drinks cupboard.

'Maureen didn't like him. She said he frightened her. He frightened me too. It got so bad that I was glad when he left the country.'

Raven looked at his friend with affection. 'Come on now, Patrick,' he said. 'There's nothing on that tape that should worry you. The man wants to talk to you. No more, no less.'

'But I don't want to talk to *him*,' the lawyer said firmly.

Raven kicked off a slipper. The carpet was warm underfoot. 'So what are you going to do? You can't go to the police. They'd just laugh at you.'

'I don't intend going to the police,' said the lawyer. 'I want you to do something about it.'

'Me?' Raven repeated.

O'Callaghan put his coffee cup down very carefully. 'I've

held your hand enough times in the past. Lied for you, risked my professional reputation. It's time for you to do something for me for a change.'

'I do believe that you're serious,' Raven said. 'OK. What exactly do you want me to do?'

'Talk to him,' the lawyer said earnestly. 'Make him listen to reason. Find out what he wants. I don't know, John. I can't handle this sort of thing.'

'Right,' Raven said briskly. 'What's his number?'

'That's part of the problem, I don't know any longer. His wife killed herself while he was in America. The house they lived in was sold. Nobody seems to know where his daughter is living. For God's sake, John. We're talking about a telephone number. That shouldn't be a problem for someone like you.'

Raven picked up the phone. The truth was that he no longer had the help he had previously since the postal services had been privatised.

He punched out seven digits. 'Is that Horseferry Road Magistrates' Court? This is the *Daily Herald*. Look, you had someone remanded on bail yesterday. Someone called Philip Page. Have you got an address for him?'

The answer was curt and righteous. 'We don't give out this sort of information.' Raven replaced the receiver.

O'Callaghan was looking at a newspaper article. He pushed it across the table. There was a picture of a fat man climbing into a limousine. The caption read: Family friend refuses to comment on Page case. The text below the picture referred to Henry Vyner, company director, of Scarclyff Manor, Shere, Surrey.

'I remember the name,' said O'Callaghan. 'Page used to mention it. Vyner's his daughter's godfather.'

Raven lifted the phone again. Directory enquiries gave him the number he needed. He dialled.

A man's voice answered. 'Scarclyff Manor.'

'I'd like to talk to Mr Vyner, please,' Raven said.

'Sorry, sir. Mr Vyner no here.'

O'Callaghan was leaning forward, doing his best to follow the conversation.

'When do you expect him back?' Raven asked.

'Some time later, sir.'

'I understand that, but when?' Raven insisted.

'After three o'clock. Good bye, sir.'

Raven picked up the coffee tray. O'Callaghan followed him into the kitchen.

'Why didn't you leave your name and number?' asked the lawyer.

Raven put the dirty cups in the sink and wiped his hands on a towel.

'Because,' he said, swinging round, 'Vyner isn't going to answer questions over the phone about his goddaughter's father and friend. I'm going to have to go down there and see him.'

O'Callaghan checked the clock on the dresser. 'I'm due in court,' he said hastily. 'So when will you go?'

'Right away,' said Raven. The adrenalin was running again. 'The thing is to get my foot in the door. I'll call you as soon as I have some news.' He helped the lawyer on with his overcoat. 'It says there that Vyner put up Page's bail.'

O'Callaghan collected his trilby. 'I'll be in the office all afternoon. For crissakes don't call me at home. Maureen mustn't know a word about this. Not a whisper, John. Is that understood?'

'Understood,' Raven said. 'You'll have to see yourself out. It's too bloody cold on deck.'

The lawyer looked at him gratefully. 'You can laugh all you want when this is over. But until then, take me seriously.'

'What else?' answered Raven. 'We're serious people here.'

He went back to the newspapers and read all he could about the Page case. Only O'Callaghan's disclosure made it interesting. Apart from that, it seemed to be just one more City scam.

He was fully dressed by the time Mrs Burrows came shuffling along the deck. He had put on a pair of cords, the black-and-red lumberjacket Kirstie had brought from Canada. He wore a pair of Duk Dry overshoes on top of his loafers.

Mrs Burrows let herself into the sitting room and stared round suspiciously. She had been cleaning the boat for sixteen years and thought of Raven's affairs as her own. She had been proud of working for a detective inspector and had been stunned by his resignation. She attributed this to a defect in character compounded by his marriage. None of Raven's ex-girlfriends had achieved live-in privileges. Raven's obsession with his new wife had given Mrs Burrows fears for his reason. She had soldiered on with a grim disapproval that was totally lost on her mistress.

Alma Burrows was a small sparrowlike woman bundled into trousers and an assortment of sweaters. Her raincoat had once belonged to Kirstie Raven. She removed most of her outer wrappings and marched straight into the kitchen. It was customary for her to have a cup of tea and a cigarette on the few occasions that she and Raven were alone together. This morning was no exception. She sat down across the table from Raven and lit one of his Gitanes.

'I just saw Mr O'Callaghan getting into a taxi at the bottom of Oakley Street.'

Raven closed the RAC handbook. He had been finding the best way to Shere.

'He was here,' he said.

She coughed, inhaled deeply and coughed again.

'You're not in no trouble, I hope?'

'No one's in trouble,' he said.

Mrs Burrows came into her own in times of calamity. If there was no current calamity she was quite happy to invent one. She wiped her left eye, inspecting him narrowly with the other one.

'You ought to get out more,' she said severely. 'It does you no good sitting here moping about. It ain't natural for a man to be by hisself for so long. Not a man like you, anyway.'

He shrugged. Kirstie had been in Canada for three weeks, visiting family and doing a series of pictures for the *Toronto Star*.

'Why don't you have people round of an evening no more?' she challenged.

'Because I'm a married man,' he replied.

'That's as may be,' she said darkly. 'I can remember. Why don't you go round to see that pretty Maggie Sanchez. Now there's an elegant lady. Fun, too, I wouldn't be surprised.'

Maggie Sanchez was a half-Spanish, half-Guatemalan model who did a lot of work with Kirstie Raven.

'She'd be glad of the company,' Mrs Burrows said slyly. 'Plus she's a friend of your wife's.'

'I'll tell you what,' Raven said. 'Why don't you take your tea through and start in the bedroom. I've got a couple of letters to write.'

She rose with hurt dignity. He heard her banging the crockery in the kitchen. Then the Hoover droned in the bedroom. He wrote a couple of cheques and put the RAC handbook back on the shelf. He pitched his voice above the noise of the Hoover.

'I'm off, Mrs Burrows. Don't bother about food for tonight. I'm out.'

She cooked food for him in Kirstie's absence. Stodgy stews and ferocious meatloafs. These he fed to the fish and the seagulls.

It was half past eleven as he reached the top of the steps outside. The massive granite blocks along the Embankment had been hewn in quarries worked by inmates of Dartmoor prison. The snow was falling in flurries without enough weight to settle. The signals changed at the south end of Oakley Street. Raven sprinted for the opposite side. The cul-de-sac was a narrow tongue of asphalt twenty yards long and just wide enough to take one car. The shop there belonged to Raven's neighbour, Hank Lauterbach. The American's double window displayed an exotic arrangement of Far Eastern junk. Brass and wood figurines from Burma and India, bolts of Thai silk, paper dragons from China. Lauterbach was dozing on a monastic throne, his feet on his Great Dane's back. Neither looked up as Raven passed.

He opened the car door on the driver's side and slid behind the wheel. The BMW 535 was the fourth car the Ravens had owned in two years. Both he and his wife knew what they wanted. The compromise was the BMW, a vehicle with style, speed and reliability.

He moved the car to the mouth of the cul-de-sac and made his way to the Portsmouth road. Once beyond Esher he turned left towards Horsham and Leatherhead. Visibility was marginally better. The gusts of wind had subsided and the snow settled gently. The dial on the dashboard showed the outside temperature to be 37° Fahrenheit. Passing traffic sprayed slush on verges and pavements alike.

It was one o'clock when he drove into an empty carpark. A sign outside the small inn read: HOT AND COLD FOOD, REAL ALE. Raven walked into a bar where a coal fire burned in the grate. Its light was reflected from the copper utensils hanging on the walls. A woman was standing behind the counter.

Raven ordered orange juice and a gammon steak cooked with pineapple. There was no one else in the bar. He sat down in a window nook and gazed across a half-acre field where a donkey nosed the snow disconsolately. The woman brought his food to the table. The gammon was overcooked, the pineapple canned. He ate without relish, his mind on Vyner. Raven's service as a police officer had steeled him against embarrassment. He would have no problem asking questions. He took his plate to the counter and reached into his pocket for money to pay.

'It's me, not your cooking,' he lied, excusing the half-eaten food. 'No appetite.'

'What a shame,' she replied. She counted out the change, looking through the window at the BMW. 'You're not from these parts?'

'No,' he admitted. 'To tell you the truth, I'm lost.'

The woman laughed. 'I thought you might be. You get to know most of the people who live in the neighbourhood. Most of those who do come are selling something. You don't look like a salesman.' She smiled, taking the edge off her criticism.

'I'm not,' Raven said, slipping his arms into the lumber-jacket. 'I'm looking for Scarclyff Manor. Do you know it at all?'

'That's Henry Vyner,' she said promptly. 'It's just up the road. He's a very pleasant gentleman. He comes in here sometimes. Is he a friend of yours?'

'No. I've never met him,' Raven admitted. 'How far is the house?'

She came to the door with him, pointing along the road. 'You see the petrol-station – where the lights are?' It was no more than a couple of hundred yards away, a two-pump affair with a tyre changing-bay. 'Go on past there for a couple of miles. Keep your eyes open for the sign on your left. It's easy enough to miss.'

She stayed at the door, watching as he drove off. He slackened speed at the garage. A boy wearing a baseball cap looked up as Raven drove by. The sign the woman had spoken of was almost hidden in the hedge. SCARCLYFF MANOR.

He turned left on to a lane that dropped between pine trees growing behind wire fences. Snow thickened the uppermost branches. The soil was scarred with rabbit warrens. Nothing moved. An elbow in the lane revealed the last of the trees. A lodge guarded a driveway. Smoke curled from the chimney. The wrought-iron entrance gates were open. The BMW bumped over the cattle grid. Raven drove on between laurel and rhododendron bushes, past a couple of grass tennis-courts, their nets removed for the winter. A small lake was totally still, a rowing-boat pulled up on the landing stage. There was a glimpse of a cobbled stableyard through an archway. The garage door was raised; a Bentley Continental was parked inside next to a Japanese hatchback. Raven stopped on the gravelled drive. In front of him was a small Jacobean manorhouse. A date was carved in the yellow stonework above the massive front door. Lights burned behind the curtained windows. As Raven walked across to the front door, he had the feeling that he was being watched. The door opened as Raven approached. The Filipino was dressed in dark-blue tunic and trousers. His smile was brilliant.

'Good afternoon.'

It was the same voice that Raven had heard on the telephone earlier. Tapestries hung on the stone walls of the hallway. There were flambeaux to light the carpeted floor and two staircases. These met at a gallery decorated with family portraits.

'My name's John Raven,' he said. 'Is there any chance of seeing Mr Vyner?'

The servant continued to smile, his upraised hand inviting Raven inside.

'Please,' he said. 'I go and see.'

He ushered Raven into a room on the right and closed the door quietly. Raven's first impression was one of style. Not his style maybe, but that of someone with a high degree of sophistication and the means to employ it.

Four eighteen-foot windows overlooked the gravelled drive in front of the house. Indigo blue velvet curtains reached to the floor. Silk cushions made each window embrasure comfortable. Applewood logs burned in an open fireplace. More wood lay in a basket. There was a Gainsborough portrait above the Italian clock on the mantlepiece, a glass-topped table bearing magazines, good silver and a carpet that matched the curtains.

The door from the hallway opened. A man in his late

forties came in. He was wearing a paisley scarf tucked into a flannel shirt, well-worn grey flannel trousers and a pair of embroidered slippers. His six-foot frame was draped with flesh. It hung from his jawline and over his belt. What was left of his hair was brushed flat above his ears. His voice was surprisingly mild.

'My servants are Filipino. I'm afraid they tend to get people's names wrong.'

Raven stood up. 'John Raven,' he said.

Vyner waved a hand. 'Please sit down, Mr Raven.' He stood in front of the fireplace in the Englishman's favourite position, his back to the flames, legs apart. 'What can I do for you?'

Raven hesitated. O'Callaghan's problem seemed remote from this urbane stranger.

'In the first place, thank you for seeing me,' Raven said. 'I'm in a somewhat embarrassing situation. I'm here on behalf of a friend, someone called Patrick O'Callaghan. He's trying to get in touch with Philip Page.'

'Philip Page,' Vyner repeated with a half-smile. 'Well, you won't find him here.'

'But you do know who I mean?'

'I know,' said Vyner.

A small pug-dog snuffled its way out from behind a curtain and made for the fire. Vyner picked it up by the scruff of the neck and returned it to where it had come from. He wiped his fingers fastidiously.

'Herbert stinks, but he's a very old friend.' Vyner was back at the fire. 'You were saying?'

'About Patrick O'Callaghan,' Raven said. 'He's a solicitor. Page was his client a few years ago.'

Vyner stopped him with uplifted hand. 'Is your wife Canadian, a photographer?'

The question took Raven by surprise. 'She's Canadian, and she is a photographer. Why do you ask?'

Vyner chuckled. 'The long arm of coincidence. My god-daughter took me to Canada House a couple of months ago.

40

There was an exhibition of your wife's work. She's a very talented lady. We talked for some time. As a matter of fact we gave her a lift back to your boat.'

Raven smiled guardedly. Coincidence always disturbed him. 'Kirstie never mentioned it,' he said.

'I can think of no reason why she should,' Vyner said good-naturedly. He moved away from the fire, rubbing the backs of his legs. 'She's not with you?'

The pug-dog was snoring gently behind the curtain.

'She's in Canada,' Raven answered. 'Seeing family and doing some work. That's the trouble. My wife is a busy lady. We don't see enough of one another.'

Vyner lowered his bulk into a chair very carefully. 'You mentioned your friend. I take it that friendship's important to you too?'

The smell of apple logs permeated the room. Raven caught a glimpse of himself in a mirror.

'You're talking about friendship between men, or what?' Raven asked.

Vyner nodded. 'Friendship between men.'

'If you can get it to work,' Raven said, 'it's probably the most important relationship there is.'

'I agree,' Vyner said thoughtfully. Then he smiled. 'I've known Philip Page all my life. We grew up within ten miles of one another, went to prep school and Eton the same years. I introduced Page to his wife. I was best man at his wedding. How much do you know about these charges he's facing?'

There was something about Vyner's manner that made Raven wonder if he was gay. A softness, a pliancy, yet beyond these, determination. Kirstie would know. Women picked up these things immediately.

'The charges?' Raven repeated. 'I don't know a thing about them – except what I've read in the press.'

'Did you know that his wife committed suicide eighteen months ago?'

Raven shook his head.

'It was a great shock to all of us,' Vyner said. 'What I'm really trying to say is that Philip's been through a very rough time. I'm doing my best to help him through it. And that includes protecting his privacy. I'm sure you'll appreciate that, Mr Raven.'

'I do indeed,' Raven said. He was not doing too well up to now. 'So let me tell you why I'm here. Page left a message on Patrick O'Callaghan's answering machine. It's not so much what he said as what O'Callaghan's reading into it. O'Callaghan's got this impression that Page thinks he made a statement to the police about the Consol Electric affair.'

'And did he?'

The idea was laughable. 'Of course not,' said Raven. 'Patrick's a balletomane, a gentle soul, not a police informer. In any case what could he say? That Page used to drop in at the office, take Patrick out for a drink? Bend his ear with stuff that was of no interest at all, at least to O'Callaghan.'

'And this is what you want to speak to Philip about?'

'Yes.'

'Would you believe me if I told you that I've no idea where Philip is at this moment?'

'No,' said Raven.

Vyner looked pained. 'Nevertheless, it's true, I assure you. Don't you think that I'd tell you? I mean, having met your wife and everything. I simply do not know where he is.'

'Come on, now,' said Raven. 'You stood his bail. You'd have to know where he's staying.'

'Not so,' Vyner insisted. 'All I did was sign the bail papers. The only people who know where Philip is at this moment are the police and his lawyers. If you really want to carry this any further, then they're the people to see. My own advice is to let it drop. Philip's in no mood to deal with hysterical solicitors.'

Raven smiled. The description would not appeal to O'Callaghan. He had a feeling that Vyner was stonewalling. He was clearly a good friend to Page and a determined liar as well. Raven glanced through the window. Falling snow almost obscured the BMW. It was time to move on.

He rose to his feet. 'Well, thank you for seeing me anyway.'

Vyner came through to the hallway and opened the front door.

'Drive carefully,' he warned, looking up at the sky. 'I'm sorry you had a wasted journey. Maybe you'll bring your wife down to see the house when she comes back?'

'We'd like that,' said Raven.

The front door was closed behind him. He ran for the car and wiped the outside of the windscreen with the side of his hand. Once at the wheel, he looked back at the drawing-room curtains. There was no one there, but he still felt that he was being watched. He switched on the fog lamps and drove into the pinewoods.

He was out of Esher by half past three. The Vodaphone began to ring on the passenger seat as Raven started the long climb up Putney Hill. He pulled in to the kerb immediately. A cop on the beat had taken his number only a month before. A mobile unit had located the BMW and booked Raven for using a phone when driving. The incident had cost Raven a fifty-pound fine and a second endorsement on his driving licence.

He picked up the Vodaphone. It was an irate Patrick O'Callaghan.

'Where the hell have you been? I've been calling you for the past two hours.'

'I've been in the country,' said Raven. 'The phone doesn't reach that far.'

'Where are you now?' the lawyer demanded.

'Halfway up Putney Hill.' Raven glanced over his shoulder. 'Opposite the crematorium.'

'Did you get Page's address?'

'Not yet.'

'How long is it going to take you to get home?'

Raven made a quick calculation. 'Half an hour if I'm lucky.'

'I'll be waiting outside the boat,' said the lawyer.

Raven crossed Wandsworth Bridge and turned south on Old Church Street. There were no lights showing in O'Callaghan's house, no car parked in the railed-off front area. He drove on and backed the BMW into the cul-de-sac. A cab was drawn up near the steps that led down to his boat. O'Callaghan emerged from the back of the cab as Raven zigzagged through the slowly moving traffic.

They descended the steps. Raven unlocked the door at the bottom. More snow had fallen since Mrs Burrows had swept the deck. Raven led O'Callaghan into the sitting room. A note was propped against Kirstie's photograph: *Mr O'Callaghan phoned three times. He said it was important.*

'You're damn right it was important,' the lawyer said, divesting himself of his overcoat. He straightened his bow tie, nervously looking into the mirror. 'Page called the office this morning.'

'What time was that?' Raven asked.

O'Callaghan gestured uncertainly. 'Some time before noon. He wouldn't give his name to Anne but insisted on talking to me.'

Raven opened the drinks cupboard and poured brandy into a glass.

'Drink this,' he said to his friend, 'and for crissakes sit down and relax.'

The lawyer obeyed, holding the glass with both hands and wagging his head. 'The bastard's going to kill me, John.'

Raven reached for his cigarettes. 'How?' he enquired.

The lawyer's face reddened. 'I don't like your tone, John. Or your manner. When are you going to start taking me seriously?'

'Now,' said Raven. 'Tell me.'

O'Callaghan put his glass down on the table. 'Page said that betrayal was something he would never accept. He said

I either withdrew the statement or suffered the consequences. I mean, that's a threat, John. A definite threat to my life.'

'The language is straight out of Dan Dare,' Raven said, smiling. 'Is any of this on tape?'

'Tape?' The lawyer was losing control of his voice. 'What do you think my office is, for God's sake? We don't tape conversations.' His eyes strayed to the brandy bottle.

Raven put it back in the cupboard and resumed his seat. 'Let's get one thing straight, Patrick. Have you ever, at any time, made a statement to the police about Philip Page?'

'Of course not,' his friend said heatedly. 'Someone from the Fraud Squad called me shortly after Page left the country. He said he wanted to ask me some questions. I explained that Page was my client, that anything that may have passed between us in conversation was privileged. Confidential. That's the last I heard of it. The police never contacted me again, nor did I go near them.'

Raven touched the button that drew the curtains, sealing the warm room against intrusion. 'Suppose the name on this statement turns out to be yours?'

The idea clearly worried the lawyer. 'Then it would have to be a forgery.'

'There has to be a name on a statement,' Raven said.

A look of resignation clouded O'Callaghan's face. 'Don't be ridiculous, John. You know as well as I do the way things are done. The police are willing to go to any lengths to protect their witnesses. Everyone knows it, including the judges. What do you suppose happens with these so-called supergrasses? You think they give their right names in court? It's what a witness says that matters, not his identity. At least that kind of witness.'

'You'd better get a hold on yourself,' Raven warned. 'OK, I accept that you're telling the truth, but you're not carrying on like a man with nothing on his conscience.'

'You don't know Page,' said the lawyer. 'This man's capable of anything.'

'I'll make some tea,' Raven said quickly.

When he came back from the kitchen, O'Callaghan was hunched forward, looking at the carpet between his feet. He took the cup Raven gave him.

'Vyner knows Kirstie,' said Raven.

O'Callaghan almost choked on his tea. 'Knows Kirstie? How do you mean?'

'Page's daughter took Vyner to an exhibition of Kirstie's work at Canada House. They gave Kirstie a lift home. They said it was on their way,' Raven said significantly.

The news brought new life to the lawyer's voice. 'You mean they live in the neighbourhood?'

Raven hooked the slice of lemon out of his cup. 'Let's look at it from Vyner's point of view. He's protecting his friend, right? He knows that half London's going to be looking for him. Nobody's sure what he's done with the money. They'll be like a plague of rats. Everyone looking for Philip Page. So where's Vyner going to put him?'

Patrick O'Callaghan felt along his jawline. 'Somewhere that no one else knows about?'

'That's right,' agreed Raven and picked up the phone. He glanced at the clock. It was almost one in the afternoon in Toronto. He punched out the number and waited. The reply came loud and clear.

'This is the MacLeod home. Kirstie Raven speaking.'

Raven pictured the old house in Toronto. Pathways cleared through the snowbanks. Miles of underground shopping malls. Handshakes charged with static electricity.

'It's me,' he said comfortably. 'How are you?'

'I'm fine.' Anxiety crept into her voice. 'Is something wrong?'

Kirstie had always been difficult to lie to. It irked Raven that lying was necessary. But Kirstie worried about him. It was as simple as that.

'I'm OK. I just wanted to hear your voice.'

'I miss you too,' she replied. Her words were riding the

wave of sound in the background. 'What have you been up to?'

'I've been helping Patrick O'Callaghan. He had a little problem.' He steered away from the subject quickly. The lawyer was one of Kirstie's favourites, but about certain things she was psychic. They killed five minutes talking about her family. Then Raven came to it.

'I met an admirer of yours the other day. An admirer of your work, that is. Someone called Henry Vyner. His goddaughter took him to Canada House for an exhibition. He says he met you there.'

She repeated the name with no sign of recognition. 'I don't recall,' she admitted.

'A fat man, like a younger version of Sydney Greenstreet?'

She laughed. 'But of course – they drove me home. How did you meet them?'

'I met him, not her,' Raven corrected. He kept his tone casual. 'He happened to mention that they lived somewhere near us. It sort of went from there.'

O'Callaghan's eyes were half closed as he listened.

'Where exactly *does* he live?' Raven asked.

'The girl lives in Dolphin Square. One of those flats. I'm not sure about him. Why do you want to know?'

'Curiosity, that's all.'

'I think it's somewhere along the Embankment,' she answered. 'Someone at the door,' she said hurriedly. 'I'll talk to you later.'

Raven dialled 192. 'Directory enquiries? Look, a friend of mine lives on Chelsea Embankment in London. I've forgotten the number. His name's Henry Vyner. Can you help at all?'

'One moment.'

Raven waited as the girl consulted the screen in front of her. Then she was back.

'I'm sorry, caller. I have no listing for a Henry Vyner in Chelsea Embankment.'

Raven replaced the handset. 'The phone's probably in somebody else's name. Don't worry, I'll cope.'

O'Callaghan was looking more cheerful. He finished what was left of his cup of tea. 'I'd better get home,' he said, rising. 'Maureen's taking the dog to the vet. She wants me to go with her.'

'Good,' said Raven. 'It'll take her mind off other things.' A thought struck him. 'Look, why don't you tell Maureen that I'm in some sort of trouble. That always goes down well. Say that you can't talk about it for obvious reasons but you are a little bit worried. It would take the heat out of the situation.'

The lawyer struggled into his astrakhan-lined overcoat. 'A good idea,' he said gratefully. 'I won't forget what you're doing, John.'

Raven opened the door. 'You will,' he said. 'It's the kick in the ass we always remember.'

O'Callaghan clapped his hat on his head. 'You think I'm a coward, don't you?'

'Nothing wrong in being a coward,' Raven smiled. 'It's the human condition. Don't worry about it. We've both done foolish and desperate things in our time.'

O'Callaghan turned up his coat collar. 'I don't like foolish and desperate things! I like to maintain control. This kind of behaviour's beyond me.'

Raven watched the lawyer to the top of the steps, shut out the cold night and pushed the bolts.

He checked his reference books for a Chelsea address for Vyner and found none. He played music until nine o'clock then listened to the BBC news on television. He ate standing up in the kitchen as he sometimes did when alone. It was almost midnight when he turned out the light. Five minutes later he was sleeping.

Chapter Three

It was still dark outside when Raven woke. He groped for the bedside radio. There was no sound other than the groans of the houseboat as it rode on the ebbing tide. The newscaster warned of more snow in the offing, ice on the roads. Raven swung his legs out of bed and opened the curtains. The view across the river was bleak. Street-lamps still shone in Battersea Park, lighting the skeletal trees and deserted paths. The snow had stopped falling, at least for the time being.

Raven donned his robe, took a stiff broom from the kitchen cupboard and cleared a path along the deck as far as the steps. He collected the newspapers. The post had not yet been delivered. He took the newspapers and a mug of strong tea back to bed. The phone rang just after nine. It was Mrs Burrows reporting a burst waterpipe. She was waiting at home for the plumber to arrive. Raven told her not to come to work, and took a very hot bath. He dressed in his long johns, flannel shirt and cords. The lumberjacket came last. He locked up the boat and started walking east along the Embankment. There were few people in sight. Bad weather had reduced the flow of traffic.

Raven crossed Oakley Street. A street cleaner dressed in yellow oilskins was sanding the pavement ahead. Raven knew him of old. The man swept between the two bridges, addressing his job with a dwindling sense of duty.

Raven touched the Irishman's shoulder. 'Good morning, Redmond.'

The man turned, his head wrapped in a grey balaclava helmet.

'It's you, is it?' he questioned morosely.

He hooked a cigarette from the packet Raven offered and lit it with mittened fingers. He spat at the spent match and missed.

'So the missus is still over the sea, is she?' he enquired through a hacking cough.

'Still away, more's the pity,' said Raven. There were only ten houses left along Chelsea Embankment.

The Irishman drew deep on his cigarette. 'Then why aren't you still in yer bed or did you piss in it?'

'Restless, Redmond,' said Raven. 'Tell me, do you know anyone in these parts called Henry Vyner?'

The Irishman spat again. 'I know Henry Vyner. Didn't he report me to the council, so he did. The pavement in front of his house was always dirty, he said. Would you believe that now? With the likes of the dirty buggers that's passing along here every day. And him seldom there in any case. He lives in the country. He's no friend of yours now, I hope?'

'No friend,' said Raven. 'An acquaintance. I can't even remember which house he lives in.'

'Number thirty-four,' the Irishman said promptly.

Raven made slow time walking as far as Chelsea Bridge. By the time he looked back, the Irishman was out of sight. Raven stopped in front of number thirty-four. He climbed the three steps. There was no nameplate. Two bells. Raven rang both.

An educated voice sounded in the entryphone. 'Who is it?'

Raven leaned into the grilled mouthpiece. 'I've got a letter for Mr Henry Vyner.'

'Push it through the letterbox,' said the voice.

'I can't do that,' Raven said. 'I need a signature.'

'OK. You'd better come up. Top floor. The lift's on your left.'

The front door clicked open, allowing Raven into a warm bright hallway with flowers on a table. The carpeted lift cage had an ornamental grille at the front. There was only one stop. The man standing at the door of the penthouse flat was wearing a polka-dotted silk robe over blue pyjamas. He had rust-coloured hair and a deep sun tan. His eyes fixed on Raven suspiciously.

Raven's smile was larger than his mouth. 'Philip Page?'

The man jerked his thumb at the lift. 'Out!' he ordered.

Raven continued to stand his ground. He could see past Page into the hallway. Pussy-willow buds sprouted from an enamelled vase.

'There's been enough trouble as it is,' Raven said quietly. 'O'Callaghan doesn't need it, nor do you. I'm here on his behalf.'

Page showed no sign of retreating either. 'Piss off!' he said shortly.

Raven's hope of settling what must have been a misunderstanding was retreating rapidly. 'You're taking liberties with a man who doesn't know how to defend himself. Look, we might as well deal with this in a civilised manner. I know who you are and where you live. I'm not going to disappear.'

Page said nothing.

'O'Callaghan didn't make that statement,' said Raven.

'I'll give you five minutes,' said Page, letting Raven into the hallway.

It was going to take longer than that, thought Raven. But at least he was inside the flat.

Page preceded him into a large room with a couple of double-glazed windows overlooking the river and the Embankment. The walls were pale blue, the room solidly masculine. It was yet another aspect of Vyner's character. There were books, magazines, a couple of French horse bronzes and a box of Mexican panatellas. A smell of burnt toast hung in the air.

'I need to use your loo,' Raven said suddenly.

'Last door on your right,' Page said, nodding towards the corridor.

There were two bedrooms, one with the door wide open. A blazer and slacks were draped on the back of a chair. More clothes hung in a walk-in wardrobe. Raven shut the door of the bathroom behind him. The half-tiled walls were decorated with pictures of soaring dolphins. The sunken bath allowed its occupant to look down at the wintry gardens of the Royal Hospital. Raven stepped over the damp towels on the floor. He could see no outside fire escape. Glass shelves were packed with oils and lotions. A woman had been here recently. There was nobody else in the flat at the moment. Raven noticed these things from habit.

He washed his hands and went back to the sitting room. Page was putting the phone down as Raven came back. Raven sat down near the artificial log fire.

'I just talked to Henry Vyner,' said Page. 'You've been down there pestering him as well. Just what do you expect to achieve by these intrusions?'

Raven had wet-combed his greying-blond hair. His face seemed to be hanging open with this insane grin on it every time he looked in the mirror. He undid the belt on his lumberjacket.

'I asked myself the same question,' he said. His varicose vein was beginning to throb again. The three-thousand-pound operation seemed to have done no more than transfer the problem. 'You're not going to say you don't know who Patrick O'Callaghan is?' he challenged.

'I'm not likely to forget him,' Page said grimly.

'He's a good friend of mine,' Raven said. 'I don't like to hear of him being threatened with violence.'

Page cocked his head. 'Is that what he told you?'

'I heard the message you left on his answering machine. It was way out of order.'

Page pushed fingers through his hair. Similarly coloured

stubble showed on his sun-tanned face. He had not yet shaved. 'You're the first Old Harrovian I ever heard of who became a cop.'

A smile crept back on Raven's face. 'I couldn't resist the uniform. And that's ex-cop. I resigned quite a few years ago. It sounds as though your friend has been doing his homework.'

'Let's get back to these so-called threats,' said Page. 'Why doesn't O'Callaghan complain to the police?'

'It wasn't that sort of threat, was it?' Raven countered.

Page lit a panatella. 'O'Callaghan has made a statement about me. It's a tissue of lies and I want it withdrawn. Nothing else. Just the statement withdrawn.'

Page blew two smoke rings, one inside the other. The accomplishment added to Raven's irritation. His wife was able to do it. He never could.

'How do you know that this statement exists?' he asked. 'Have you seen it?'

Page had a trick of hanging his head as he listened, bringing it up sharply when the speaker had finished.

'I don't *have* to see it,' he said. 'I've heard some of the shit it contains. Do you take milk and sugar?'

Raven blinked.

'I'll make some coffee,' said Page.

He came back from the kitchen, carrying two cups. He gave one to Raven. 'O'Callaghan's your friend so he can't be an asshole – is that how it goes?'

Raven found himself pursing his lips and attempting to emulate Page's smoke rings. No good. He leaked a smile, covering his discomfiture. 'Patrick denies having anything to do with a statement. He never even saw the police.'

Page leaned forward. It was as though he viewed Raven afresh. 'Do you want to hear the truth about this? Or aren't you really interested?'

'Tell me,' said Raven. 'It's what I came for.'

Page tightened the sash of his robe, a wrestler preparing

for combat. He was on his feet now, pacing. He came to a sudden stop and swung round.

'I'll try to keep this as short as I can. If there's something you don't understand, say so.'

Raven waved a hand. Now he was doing better than he had expected.

Page lowered himself back in his chair, his eyes on Raven. 'It started four years ago. Those were the days when I gambled. I met this Pakistani in Crockford's. He was a colonel in their air force, an attaché in London. He was Sandhurst-educated, amusing. We had drinks together, a few meals, then he disappeared. He surfaced again four months later with the news that he'd changed his job. He'd been appointed chief of a Pakistani air force purchasing commission. They were interested in gun sights for night bombers. Are you with me so far?'

Raven nodded.

'I'd heard about this company near Reading. Pantile HiTek. It was a family-run firm that had done work for the Saudis. They were going through a cashflow problem. I talked to Ferook about it and we went down to see the plant. Ferook said it would work. I borrowed the money from the bank and bought Pantile HiTek, lock, stock and barrel.' He put his cup down and wiped his mouth on the back of his hand.

Raven eased the pain in his left calf. 'By now you're in business with Ferook, is that it?'

'Clandestinely,' Page corrected. 'Ferook couldn't afford to be directly involved with me. The first contract he was offering was worth millions. There'd be others.'

Raven whistled, a long dropping note like a starling.

Page shook his head. 'That's not a lot of money for those people. Anyway, that was the state of affairs. As I said, I'd bought Pantile HiTek with money that I got from the bank. Now my first deal was going to make me four times as much. I pay off the bank and Ferook gets his points.'

He came to his feet again as though pained by the recollection.

'Do you understand anything at all about the world of arms dealing?'

'Not a lot,' Raven admitted. 'Only what I read. Khashoggi and people.'

Page raised a finger. 'You've got to understand how these things are done. These deals are made on a nod and a handshake. The basis is mutual trust and mutual greed. Everyone operates under a blanket of confidentiality. This is where Consol Electric comes into the picture. They were anxious to expand. Rumours were already going round about the Pakistani contract. Consol Electric made me an offer I couldn't refuse. Fourteen million for Pantile HiTek plus whatever contracts were on their books.'

Raven leaned back. There was something childlike about the other man's need to explain. 'By now you had the contract in your possession?'

'No,' said Page. 'I had Consol Electric's cheque. They had my company but the contract was still in Pakistan awaiting two signatures. Consol Electric knew all about this at the time. They'd gone against the advice of their merchant bankers and backed their own hunch. Once again, greed.' He dwelt on the word, jaw muscles tightening.

'What happened next?' Page asked the question rhetorically. 'General Zia gets himself blown out of the sky with Ferook and some others. Bhutto's elected and repudiates all arms deals made by the old regime. What was I supposed to do – return Consol Electric's money? I'd made that deal in good faith.'

Raven offered no comment. Something odd had happened during the last half hour or so. He was no longer a stranger. Page was confiding in him. There was no question about the man's sincerity. He was desperately anxious that Raven should hear his side of things.

'All hell broke loose,' said Page. 'Consol Electric were

55

shouting their heads off. The Department of Trade and Industry moved in, then the Fraud Squad. Reporters were camping outside my house. I had a seventeen-year-old daughter at school, a wife who was drinking. I packed a bag and took off.'

'Leaving your wife and daughter behind?'

Page moved his head in assent. 'My marriage was over by then. It was over the moment my daughter was born. I wanted to take Drusilla with me. But that would have meant leaving my wife alone.' He shrugged. 'I just couldn't do that to her.'

Raven crushed his cigarette into the ashtray. 'That's life.' It was all he could think of to say.

Page was in full flow by now. 'I made no secret about what I was doing. I used my own passport to leave the country. The ticket was booked in my name. No one prevented me leaving. Anyway, a couple of years went by. I'd bought this place in Carmel Valley by then. The FBI drove out to the ranch early one morning with a warrant for my extradition. The case was chucked out because of insufficient evidence.'

Page broke off suddenly. He went into the kitchen and came back holding a glass of mineral water. Raven understood that at last he was being asked to comment. It was difficult without giving offence.

'What happened to your family?' he asked.

'Henry Vyner took care of them for me. He bought the lease on a flat in Dolphin Square and paid the school fees at Saint Mary's, Ascot. Then I heard that Marian had killed herself. Vyner told me not to come back for the funeral. I wouldn't have gone in any case. The Brits were still trying to get hold of me. I went on living my life, breeding a few horses, fishing. I should have known that the Brits don't give up that easily. Not where money's involved. The FBI arrived at my place again, this time with a new warrant. This time it was backed by what they claimed was an important new statement. I was in and out of federal court within three hours.'

'And back here,' said Raven. 'And was all this because of the statement?'

'That's right,' agreed Page. 'A statement by someone who was supposed to have been with me at the time I was doing the deal with Consol Electric. I'm supposed to have told this man that the Pakistani contract was a con. That it would never materialise. This bastard gave details of my movements, the people I talked to. It was a very cunning mixture of fiction and fact, enough to get me back to this country. And now it's going to bury me.'

Raven shifted on the couch. 'Are you saying that there was no name on this statement?'

'I'm saying it was never mentioned in open court. The statement was never read in full, just bits of it.'

'What happened to the money you took?' The words were out before Raven could stop them.

Page's face was expressionless. After a while he smiled. 'I banked it,' he said.

Raven grinned in spite of himself. The other man's manner was hard to resist, a frank appeal to be heard before being judged. Raven was trying to work out the interest on the money involved. It was more than he'd ever need or for that matter want.

'Let's get back to O'Callaghan,' Raven said. 'You haven't produced one single reason to show me he's responsible. I've known him for more than twenty years. He's got no time for the police. He won't even prosecute. He's a gentle and sensitive man born out of his time. Betrayal is totally foreign to his nature.'

'Your loyalty could be misplaced,' Page suggested.

'I doubt it,' said Raven. 'Most of what you said to him he can't even remember. He just wasn't interested. It may come as a blow to your ego, but it's true. I mean, look at things logically. What would his motive be?'

Page made a sound of impatience. 'Don't be naive. Consol Electric's a multi-national company. They have worldwide interests. They're in a position to do favours for someone like Patrick O'Callaghan.'

'These papers you're supposed to have shredded, what were they?'

Page took the question to the window and turned. 'Notes about phone calls I'd made to Colonel Ferook. Cables from Pakistan. Stuff that in the wrong hands could damage me. I had no time to destroy them myself. My wife said she'd do it for me.'

'And did she?'

Page lifted his shoulders. 'Nobody seems to know what happened. You've got to understand the position. The authorities were blocking the sale of our house in Chesham Street. She had to move quickly. Henry Vyner took care of everything. He bought the flat for her and Drusilla, dealt with the nuns at Saint Mary's. He even tried to control Marian's drinking. He never saw any papers.'

Raven was suddenly aware of an anomaly. He found himself admiring Page's defiance, his readiness to go down fighting. Raven had no certainty of the other man's guilt or innocence. Nevertheless, Raven's own experiences with Scotland Yard put him on Page's side instinctively.

'You know what?' Raven said. 'We both want the same thing but for different reasons. You want this statement withdrawn. I want you off my friend's back. We should be helping one another, not fighting.'

Page looked at him closely. 'I'm not sure I'm with you.'

'It's simple enough,' Raven said. 'I can be useful. I still have the right contacts.'

'That's not what Vyner says,' Page replied. He was smiling. 'According to him you're not too popular at Scotland Yard.'

'I don't know where he's getting his information,' said Raven, 'but it's wrong. I still have friends. With a little bit of luck I can find out whose name's on the statement.'

'And if it turns out to be Patrick O'Callaghan's?'

'It won't,' Raven said with assurance. 'But if it should turn out to be Patrick, I'll guarantee that the statement's withdrawn.'

Page thought about it, his forehead furrowed. 'Do you think you could do that?'

'I've done it before,' Raven said. 'You've got, what, a couple of months before going for trial? All I want is a week of it. A seven days' truce. During that time I go to work and you stay away from O'Callaghan.'

Page stared at the snowflakes melting on the windowpane. His expression was undecided.

'You're in no position to bargain,' urged Raven. 'How many people have you talked to about all this?'

'Only Henry Vyner, that's all.'

'And what does he say?'

Page dragged his gaze back to Raven. 'As I told you, I've known Henry for most of my life. But it's not easy sometimes to know what he's thinking. Most of the time he just listens.'

'What about your daughter?'

'I haven't had the chance to talk to her yet.' He shrugged and half smiled. 'It's going to be difficult. She was very close to her mother.'

'Look,' Raven said, 'let's get one thing straight. I don't give a shit whether or not you ripped off Consol Electric. My only concern is for Patrick O'Callaghan.'

The two men stared into one another's eyes for half a minute. Then Page pushed out his hand. 'It's a deal.'

'OK,' said Raven. 'Let's start again. How many other people are there who could have informed against you? People who would know the details in that statement?'

'Apart from O'Callaghan? Only one. And he's in no position to open his mouth. But he still might have done.'

'How do you mean?'

'There was this guy working for Consol at the time they

took me over. He was Consol's financial adviser. He bought their stock on the side, took a ride up with it and dropped off before the balloon exploded. That was insider dealing, a criminal offence even then. I know what he did and he knows that I know.'

'What's his name?' Raven asked.

'Marcus Poole.' Page looked up from studying his knuckles. 'I thought we'd be using your contacts.'

'We are,' Raven assured him. 'But I'd still like an address if you've got one.'

Page went into the bedroom. He came back with a visiting card.

Marcus Poole

Investment Consultant

Pitt Court

273 St James's Street, S.W.1.

'He bought the building when he left Consol Electric,' Page explained. 'He lives up in the penthouse.'

'Have you been in touch with him since you got back here?' asked Raven.

'One phone call,' said Page. 'The same sort of thing as with O'Callaghan. I left a message on his answering machine.'

'You really go at it, don't you?' said Raven. It was half past ten. He had been in the flat for more than an hour. A limited trust seemed to have developed between them. It still had to be justified.

He touched Page's shoulder. 'Come over here for a minute.' They stood at the window.

Raven pointed at the flotilla of houseboats upstream. They were almost obscured by the snow.

'I live on the first boat,' Raven said. 'It's called the *Albatross*. If you need me in a hurry and I'm not around, you can leave a message with my neighbour. He's got a shop in the cul-de-sac opposite.'

Page opened the door to the landing. A Hoover droned on the floor below.

'OK,' he told Raven. 'I'm relying on you. I hope you're as good as you say you are.'

'I'm better,' said Raven, closing the cage. The flat door closed as the lift began its descent.

Chapter Four

The snow was blowing straight into Raven's face as he walked back towards the boats. Traffic cut swathes in the slush. The temperature had dropped noticeably since early morning. It took care to go down the slippery steps. He let himself in, hung the lumberjacket up to dry and slumped on the couch.

The depth and strength of Page's feelings impressed him. Raven lifted the phone. Jerry Soo and he had been to police college together. Out of step with the other cadets, they had bonded a friendship that had survived Raven's maverick behaviour and eventual resignation. The Hong-Kong-born cop could be critical but never disloyal. The two men shared a masochistic liking for standing thigh-deep in water and fishing for salmon, beset by ferocious midges.

A man's voice came on the line. 'CI5, Hogan speaking.'

'Is Jerry Soo there?'

'I'm sorry, Superintendent Soo's not available.' There was a touch of impatience in the man's tone.

'Have you any idea when he will be available? I'm a personal friend of his.'

'He's away on a course. I've no idea when he's due back.'

The connection was broken.

Raven left a message on the O'Callaghans' answering machine. It was carefully phrased.

'I've seen the party concerned and we've reached an arrangement. I'll talk to you later.'

He looked at his watch. If he hurried he should catch Marcus Poole before lunch. A frontal attack would be best. This was no time for fancy footwork. He chose a grey flannel suit from the wardrobe in the bedroom. He had only four suits left on the hangers. Kirstie had donated the others to Oxfam. He added an unaccustomed tie to the pink shirt that completed his attire. His hair needed cutting. They said that the older you got, the faster your hair grew.

He donned his Burberry and called Kirstie's cab service. 'I'd like a taxi please, going from Chelsea Embankment to St James's. It's on account and the name is Raven.' He gave the despatcher his address and telephone number.

It wasn't like Jerry Soo to leave town without letting Raven know. He was the only one left at the Yard whom Raven could ask for help. The phone rang. The cab was outside. It was one of the new models with an advertisement for a mortgage broker on the side and added space at the back.

Raven pulled the door shut. A blast of hot air assailed his neck and his ankles. The cab driver screwed his head round until he had Raven's reflection fixed in the rear-view mirror.

'St James's Street, is it?'

Raven nodded.

'I just come from Piccadilly,' the driver volunteered. 'Traffic's blocked solid from Hyde Park Corner. You want to go through the park?'

'Whatever,' said Raven. 'And will you please turn the heat down?'

The roar stopped in the air vents. The only sound left in the cab came from a transistor propped on the dashboard. The man seemed to drive with his chin, head turning with the movement of the steering wheel. It was twenty to one as they passed through the arch of St James's Palace.

Pitt Court was a block of flats on the corner across the street. A dark-blue Corniche was parked in front of the entrance. The limousine was fitted with vanity plates. OMP 1.

Raven paid the driver and went through the plate-glass entrance door. There was a narrow hallway lined with mirrors, a lift next to the staircase. A man dressed in porter's uniform was sitting behind a counter. A deaf aid peeped from his left ear.

Raven raised his voice. 'Mr Poole?'

The porter nodded across at the lift. 'Third floor, flat number six.'

The lift rose rapidly. Raven stepped out into a corridor brightened with flowers. Number six was on his right. He pushed the door open. A tall girl was sitting at a table, reading a copy of *Vogue*. She rose to her feet. She was in her early twenties with shoulder-length blonde hair. Her sun tan was as deep as Page's. Her short black skirt finished eighteen inches above her knees. She was wearing an orange shirt with gold cufflinks.

'Can I help you?' she asked, smiling.

There was no office furniture, just a few chairs, a couch and a couple of Persian rugs. A joint burned in the ashtray.

'I'm here to see Marcus Poole,' said Raven.

She stared at him disbelievingly. 'Are you sure?'

Raven made a face. 'What makes you say that? I have come to the right address, haven't I?'

'Oh yes,' she said quickly. 'It's just that I don't have your name in the book. In any case, Marcus hasn't been down yet this morning.'

'How do you mean "down"?' Raven queried.

'He lives up in the penthouse. He doesn't come into the office every day.'

Raven cocked his head, intrigued by her accent. 'Where do you come from?' he asked.

'Sweden. Have you ever been there?'

'Before you were born,' he said, remembering. 'It was some beach just outside Stockholm. A nudist beach where people walked into freezing water stark naked. Goosebumps and blue appendages.'

The anecdote left her unmoved. 'I've got strict orders about disturbing Marcus, especially in the morning. He meditates.'

Raven leaned down over the table. 'You're going to have to disturb him. Tell him it's the police.'

Her hand flew to her mouth. She stubbed out the roach in the ashtray.

'My God!' she said. 'You are a policeman?'

'Just call him,' said Raven.

She picked up the house phone, swung her chair round and spoke with her back to Raven.

'Marcus? There's a man here from the police. Downstairs in the office. He says that he wants to see you.' She spoke for a couple more minutes.

'Can I get you some tea or coffee?' He shook his head. She opened the door to an inner room. 'Please make yourself comfortable,' said the girl. She was still looking apprehensive.

This was a larger room with silk-draped windows and a suede-covered sofa. A large TV set stood on a low Chinese table. Dominating the wall was a photograph of a fat shaven-headed man in a saffron robe, sitting cross-legged.

The door opened again. The newcomer was six inches shorter than Raven with a full head of springy grey hair and a matching beard and moustache. He wore an Italian suit, open-necked shirt and a pair of snakeskin loafers. He looked at Raven, his expression curious.

'I'm Marcus Poole. I understand that you're from the police?'

'That's what I told your friend,' Raven answered. 'I wanted to make sure you'd see me. I'm a friend of Philip Page's.'

It was a while before Poole found his voice. 'Has Page sent you here?'

Raven made sure that the door was properly closed before answering. 'Are you going to testify against him?'

The question transformed Poole's face. His forehead reddened. His lips parted but no sound emerged. He swallowed hard and regained use of his vocal chords.

'Testify? I haven't the first idea what you're talking about. Who are you, anyway?'

Raven sensed the fear in the other man's voice. 'You made a statement to the police, didn't you?' he challenged.

Poole licked his lips cautiously. 'A statement about what?'

'About Philip Page and Consol Electric.'

The flush had subsided in Poole's face. He was steadier. 'I never even saw the police. Some people did come from the Department of Trade and Industry, but there was very little that I could tell them.'

'Really?' said Raven. 'I thought you were financial adviser at Consol Electric.'

'I was,' answered Poole. 'My advice was ignored. I resigned.'

Raven paid no heed to the other man's growing confidence. 'So if someone says that you made a statement to the police about Page, that would be wrong. Is that what you're saying?'

'Totally untrue,' snapped Poole. He looked even harder at Raven. 'Who are you, anyway? Some sort of enquiry agent? Is that what all this is about?' Indignation fired his next outburst. 'There are limits to what you people can do, you'll find. I'm not so sure that I shouldn't call the police now and let them deal with it.'

Raven had the door half open. 'You're too smart to do that. Concentrate your mind. It could be to your advantage. And when you've had time to think, call me.' He placed a card on the table. 'Here's my name and address. I'll be at home all evening.'

The blonde looked up nervously as he appeared. The ashtray in front of her had been emptied.

'Nice to have talked to you,' Raven said pleasantly.

It was still snowing outside. Raven stepped into a payphone. Philip Page answered.

'Poole could be our man,' said Raven. 'I just left him.'

'What happened?'

'I'll tell you later,' said Raven. 'In the meantime it's important that you don't go anywhere near him. I've got a feeling. Just don't do anything foolish.'

Chapter Five

It had stopped snowing during the night. A wintry sun showed through dirty windowpanes. The room was just big enough to accommodate a broken-backed single bed, a plain wooden table, a chair and a wardrobe. The bathroom was on the opposite side of the landing. There were four bathrooms in the house, one on each floor. All had the same spartan fittings. The lavatories had warped plastic seats, rolls of toilet paper propped on the window ledges. The bathtubs were stained, the linoleum cracked. Notices hanging on the backs of doors referred to the entertainment of guests after hours, and the use of unauthorised electrical appliances. The rooming-house catered for foreign students and transients. It was two hundred yards from Sloane Square.

Paolo Rossi had been there four days. He had chosen the place deliberately. There was a constant stream of people coming and going. The window in his room overlooked the back of the house with a ten-foot drop to cobblestones. These were matters that could make the difference between life and death.

Rossi was twenty-eight years old and stockily built with dark-brown hair and eyes. He was lying on the bed in his shorts, a cigarette burning in the ashtray beside him. By raising his shoulders he had a clear view of the mews where the Renault was parked. He had bought it from a used-car lot in Hammersmith. The bodywork was poor but the motor still functioned. It was just another expendable vehicle.

Rossi had been on the run for ten years. He had joined the Anarchist movement as a student of law at Rome University, and had directed a series of armed raids on banks and jewellery stores, using the proceeds in support of his cause. His attack on a small bank in Bolzano went badly wrong when a guard was shot dead. Two of Rossi's confederates were arrested. Rossi escaped into Austria, shedding blood and political belief as he went. During the next five years he killed nine men in different countries. None of the victims was known to him. By this time his only incentive was money.

He moved his feet to the floor and made instant coffee on the burner next to the sink. He drank, standing behind the net curtains and watching the mews. What remained of the snow had been frozen into discoloured mounds on the cobblestones. He wrapped a towel round his waist and padded across the landing. The bathroom was empty. He shaved by touch in the tub, an ability acquired through experience. Back in his room, he dragged the Samsonite case from under the bed. He undid the two combination locks. Inside were socks and underwear, a couple of drip-dry white shirts. He pulled one of these out and threw his soiled linen into a bag for the launderette. A Beretta Model Eight was concealed under the clothing. He inspected the slide mechanism and checked the eight rounds in the magazine. That done, he returned the bag to its place under the bed and donned his clean shirt. He added a tie. The man he was going to see was reported as having been involved with the death of Calvi, the papal banker. As such, he demanded respect.

Rossi belted his long black raincoat and searched the pockets. The International Driving Licence bore his photograph and passed close inspection in any country other than Italy. He let himself out of the house and walked round to the mews. The Spanish passport he had used to enter the UK was in a locker at Victoria Station. The key to the locker was taped to the bedsprings.

A parking ticket was attached to the Renault windscreen.

Rossi crumpled the piece of paper and dropped it in a nearby rubbish bin. He had collected five such tickets since he had bought the car. He drove to South Kensington and left the Renault in a metered space. He walked the last hundred yards to his destination.

'The Europa School of Languages' was above a travel agency on Old Brompton Road. Swarthy students clustered around the entrance. Arabic was the commonest tongue heard. Rossi pushed his way through the crowd and climbed five flights to the top of the building. A door with an inset optic barred his way. He rang the bell with gloved finger. Gloves had become part of his daily attire. The door opened.

Professor Aldo Frascati was a man of aristocratic appearance. White hair and eyebrows lent distinction. He was wearing a scholastic gown over his street clothes. He hurried Rossi inside and locked the door.

'You are punctual,' Frascati said with approval. They spoke in Italian, Frascati with a Sicilian accent.

'I am professional,' replied Rossi. As a Roman he had a low regard for Sicilians, referring to them privately as Africans.

He took the chair indicated. Frascati sat opposite. The small room served as an office. There was a framed certificate of merit from the Department of Education, a couple of metal filing cabinets and two shelves of textbooks.

The professor fixed his visitor with questioning eyes. 'Have you been to Pitt Court?'

The younger man nodded. 'I was there last night. The fire escapes at the back of the building are useless. There is no way to open them from the outside.'

A flicker of doubt showed in Frascati's regard. 'We cannot afford a mistake. There will be no second chance.'

Rossi maintained his show of regard for his host. 'With respect, signor,' he said evenly, 'I cannot afford a mistake. This will succeed.'

Frascati drew white eyebrows together. 'He will attend the

Maharashi Hoti Meditation centre at eight o'clock tonight. The address is 290 Holland Park Road. His car is a dark-blue Rolls-Royce, registration MP 1. He will leave at about nine o'clock and return to Pitt Court. Have you been to the restaurant?'

'Twice,' Rossi said. 'It is no more than fifty metres from the flat. There is a building under reconstruction between them.'

Frascati nodded.

Rossi spoke quietly. 'Am I allowed to ask a question, signor?'

Frascati's smile was tolerant. He clearly believed his own reputation. 'If you think it is necessary.'

'My liberty is at risk,' Rossi answered. 'You make a point of saying that there will only be one chance. It is important to me to have confidence. This visit to the Meditation Centre, the business with the restaurant trolley. How reliable is this information?'

'Unassailable,' said Frascati. 'The information comes from the Swedish secretary.'

He put his hand under his robe and withdrew a fat envelope. This he placed on his knees.

Rossi fiddled with his tie, avoiding looking at the envelope. 'I am satisfied.'

'Bravo!' Frascati said with approval. He had the indulgence of an uncle considering some juvenile prank. He opened the envelope, revealing a sheaf of bills.

'Twenty thousand United States dollars. Perhaps you would like to count them?'

Rossi stuffed the envelope in his pocket, the contents uncounted. Style was as important as respect.

Frascati's eyes were without expression. 'Call me here as soon as the matter is taken care of. I will make arrangements for the rest of the money to be paid. You are living in London?'

'Yes,' said Rossi. 'Do I have your permission to leave? There are things to be done.'

Frascati spoke words of encouragement. Rossi ignored them. These men knew nothing of danger.

'*A riverderci*!' he said and went down the stairs. He drove back to Draycott Place, collected the key to the locker and headed for Victoria Station. The continental side was crowded. Students with backpacks sprawled on the dirty floor. Women attempted to deal with fractious children. All awaited the next boat-train departure. The four rows of lockers were at the far end of the concourse. Rossi used his key and deposited the money-filled envelope.

He walked outside to the Renault. The gun was in the boot, concealed in the well of the spare wheel. He went into a hardware store on Wilton Street and bought a roll of industrial adhesive tape and a large plastic bag. The occasional gust of wind chased snow from the roofs to the street below.

Back in his room, Rossi returned the locker key to its hiding-place. He stretched out on the bed, his head hanging over the side, and considered his options. He had learned to do without friends. His sexual needs were resolved without resort to emotion. His parents had died within days of one another, shortly after his flight from Italy. He had not dared attend either funeral. His surviving relative was a married sister living in Bologna. His only link with her consisted of guarded telephone calls, all made when her husband was at work. It was four years since he had last seen her. She had no idea where or how he survived.

He lifted his head back on the pillows and stared at the ceiling. Killing had become a way of life for him. He treated each assignment as if it would be the last, obeying the basic rules for survival. There were no moral values involved as far as he was concerned. The universe was a place of continued and ruthless struggle. Any other view was unrealistic.

Street-lamps came on in the mews below. He pulled on his trousers and donned his jacket. His pockets were empty except for keys and one hundred pounds in twenties. He draped his raincoat round his shoulders like a cape and smoothed his gloved fingers. Chamois skin was both strong and supple, allowing full use of the fingers. Down in the mews, he took the gun from the boot of the Renault and stuffed it into his waistband.

Seven forty-seven p.m. Rossi found a place to park at the end of Pall Mall. He had a clear view of the lower half of St James's Street and the front of Pitt Court. The one-way flow of traffic went north up to Piccadilly. Rossi dropped still lower in his seat, concentrating on the dark-blue Rolls-Royce parked in front of the block of flats. A man came through the glass doors from the lobby. Rossi recognised him from the photograph he had been given.

Marcus Poole unlocked the Rolls and settled himself behind the wheel. The porter emerged from the lobby, carrying a couple of chairs. The rear lights of the Rolls disappeared round the corner. The porter placed the chairs in the space vacated, ensuring that nobody else could park there.

Rossi stepped out of the Renault, still hiding the gun in his waistband. He was wearing a white shirt and black trousers under his raincoat. He started walking up St James's Street, carrying the rolled-up plastic bag and industrial tape. As he came abreast of the scaffolded building, he moved sideways into the shadows there. An unlocked door led to a small yard between a brick wall and the side of the building under repair. The yard had been used as a latrine. A dead pigeon lay on the ground among scaffolding clips, empty cigarette packets and discarded fast-food containers. Vast sheets of plastic were attached to the scaffolding like sails to rigging. Enough light came from the rear of Pitt Court for Rossi to see what he was doing. He had climbed the wall on the previous night and checked out the fire escapes. It was impossible to open them from the outside. The curtains were drawn up in the penthouse. Lamps shone behind them.

Rossi dropped the roll of tape and the rubbish bag on the ground and peeped through the crack in the door. A lamp-post stood between the Girasole Restaurant and the block of flats. The circle of light it threw stopped short of where Rossi was standing. Rossi walked back to the Renault. Six minutes past nine. The Rolls came through from the park and stopped in front of Pitt Court. Poole sounded the horn. The porter hurried out and removed the chairs from the parking space. He waited until the Rolls had been moved to the kerb, picked up the chairs and followed Poole through the glass doors.

Rossi folded his raincoat and placed it on the passenger seat. It was cold on the street without his jacket. He waited in the shadows in front of the scaffolding. A waiter came out of the Girasole Restaurant, pushing a four-wheeled trolley. A thermal quilt covered the dishes. Waiter and trolley came into the light from the lamp-post. The waiter had on a white shirt and black bow tie. He wore an apron over his trousers. He moved towards Rossi, his face pinched with cold.

Rossi hissed from the darkness.

The waiter came to a halt, peering towards the scaffolding. He stiffened as Rossi came out of the shadows. Rossi held the gun to the waiter's neck and pushed him into the yard. The waiter's face grew old and afraid as Rossi put weight on the gun-barrel. The man's bow tie was on a length of elastic. Rossi removed it.

'The apron,' he said in Italian. The waiter gave it to him. 'Down on your knees,' Rossi ordered. The waiter struggled to a kneeling position.

Rossi taped the man's mouth, wrists and ankles. Then he dropped the black plastic bag over the waiter's head and shoulders, making an effective strait-jacket. Rossi pushed him forward so that he lay on the ground, face down.

Rossi stepped out, wearing the bow tie and apron. The nearest people on the street were fifty yards away. He pushed the trolley as far as the glass entrance doors. The porter glanced up from his newspaper. A radio was playing on the counter. Rossi nodded and pushed the trolley into the lift. He heard the porter speaking on the house phone.

'Your food's on the way up, Mr Poole!'

There was little enough room in the lift with the trolley. Rossi stood sideways and pressed the top button. When the lift door slid back again, Rossi saw that the door to the penthouse was open. A smell of incense came from inside the flat. The trolley wheels made no sound on the carpet as Rossi pushed the trolley forward. Poole was reclining in front of a large television screen, holding a glass of red wine in his right hand. Rossi could see the back of his head above the couch. The orange curtains were still closed.

Poole spoke without turning. 'Come back in an hour's time.'

Rossi withdrew the gun from his waistband. Two steps took him to the couch. He placed the barrel against Poole's head and blew his brain apart. Rossi slipped the gun into his trouser pocket and walked out to the landing. He pulled the door shut and stepped into the lift. There was a faint smell of burnt cordite but the noise of the shot had been lost in the soundproofed building.

The porter yawned as Rossi came from the lift. The Italian kept going. Once on the street, he pulled off the bow tie and apron. He dropped these in a rubbish bin and looked back from the Renault. There was no sign of pursuit or alarm.

Rossi drove circumspectly, heading for a deserted stretch of the Embankment between Chelsea and Fulham. Lights traced the outline of the bridges. The snowfall had stopped. The river looked cold. Rossi stopped the car and walked to the parapet. He glanced right and left and opened his hand. The gun dropped like a stone through the water below. He went through the Renault, making sure that nothing had been left under the seats or in the glove compartment. He had paid for the car in cash, and the insurance cover showed a false name. He relied on nobody else when he worked.

He used a payphone near by. Frascati answered.

'It is done,' Rossi said.

'*Va bene.*' Frascati sounded completely unmoved. 'Where are you speaking from?'

'It is close to the river.'

'Do you know where Sloane Square is?'

'Yes.' It was a short distance from where Rossi was staying.

'There is a theatre on the east side of the square with some steps in front of it. I will be there in thirty minutes. Wait for me.'

Rossi went back to the car. He turned off after half a mile and came to a halt on a side street. There was nothing behind him. He drove north as far as the King's Road and into Sloane Square. People were window-shopping in spite of the cold. He pulled to the kerb in front of the theatre. Strobe lights ran across the awning, publicising the names of the cast. The foyer was empty, the show in progress.

Rossi lit a cigarette. It was a few minutes before Frascati appeared, attired in a tailored grey overcoat and a wide-brimmed hat. Rossi had the feeling that the older man had been lurking in the underground station. Rossi opened the passenger door. Frascati looked both ways before climbing into the car.

'No problems?' he asked, smiling.

'No problems,' said Rossi.

'And the weapon?'

'Disposed of,' said Rossi. Twenty thousand dollars made a sizeable package. Frascati showed no sign of carrying it.

'Have you brought my money?' said Rossi.

Frascati's smile widened. 'We are going to collect it now. The man is pleased. He offers more work.'

Rossi pitched what was left of his cigarette through the half-open window.

'I need no more work. I have no desire to remain in this country. All I want is my money.'

The top half of Frascati's face was concealed under the hat brim. 'You shall have it. You have fulfilled all expectations.

That is why the man wants to see you. He is a man of importance who merits respect.'

Rossi's jaw muscles tightened. 'I know all about respect. The word does not mean submission.'

Frascati lifted his head. 'You will see him or you will not be paid. Those are my instructions.'

Rossi shrugged and switched on the engine. 'Where do we go?'

Frascati acted as pilot, steering Rossi through Holland Park and Shepherd's Bush. He called a halt halfway along Goldhawk Road. A ten-storey building loomed on their left. SHORT AND LONG-TERM PARKING. A two-way ramp climbed the edifice.

Rossi looked up at it. 'What happens here?' he asked, mystified.

'He meets us,' Frascati said smoothly. 'Drive to the top floor.'

Rossi moved the Renault to the foot of the ramp. A television camera picked up the time of arrival and details of number plates. There was no physical check until departure. There was an air of disuse on the top floor. Stored cars were shrouded in dust sheets. Others had notices stuck on their windscreens. There were two lifts next to an emergency staircase.

Rossi turned off the engine. Frascati moved quickly, pulling an automatic pistol from his overcoat pocket. Rossi lunged forward. The shot severed his right forefinger and smacked through the front of his skull.

Frascati scrambled out of the car as Rossi pitched sideways, his face bright with blood. Frascati stripped off Rossi's gloves and pushed the gun into Rossi's limp fingers. Frascati dropped a newspaper into the Renault and shut the passenger door. The newspaper was three days' old and showed a picture of Philip Page being escorted off a Boeing 747.

Frascati crossed the oil-stained concrete and made his way down the emergency stairs to the street.

Chapter Six

The door buzzer sounded. Raven and Philip Page looked at one another. Raven raised his shoulders and crossed the room to the entryphone.

'Who is it?'

'Police. Detective Superintendent Manning. Is that Mr Raven?'

'Yes, it is,' Raven said. 'What can I do for you?'

'I'd like to have a few words if that's possible.'

Raven pressed the door-release button. 'It's Manning,' he said.

Page was halfway out of his seat. Raven pushed him down again. 'Relax and let me do the talking.'

Raven opened the door to the deck. Cold air stiffened the hairs in his nostrils. The temperature was falling again. Half-melted icicles were refreezing. The man who stepped from the gangway came forward, a hand extended.

'I'm glad you could see me.' He peered past Raven into the sitting room. He was wearing an unbuttoned tweed overcoat, a trilby hat with a burn in the brim. He scraped the soles of his laced black shoes before stepping inside. His face assumed a look of false joviality as he saw Page.

'Well, well!' he said, wagging his head. 'I didn't expect to find you here.' He turned towards Raven who was closing the door. 'I didn't even know you two knew one another.'

Page's face showed his animosity. He was wearing a dark flannel suit and pink tie.

'Superintendent Manning, the officer in charge of my case,' he said, grudgingly.

Raven flapped a hand at a chair. Manning sat down, his feet close together.

'Who do you want to see?' Raven asked. 'Him or me?'

'You,' Manning answered. 'It might be better if we talked in private.'

'There's no need for that,' said Raven. 'Mr Page is a friend. Whatever you've got to say can be said in front of him.' His hunch was that Manning had known Page was aboard, might well have followed him earlier. 'What's your problem, Superintendent?'

'You're sure?' Manning pressed.

'What did you say?' Raven asked.

'I asked if you're sure. I mean, about talking in front of somebody else.'

'I already told you,' said Raven. 'There's no need for secrecy.'

The detective picked a shred of lint from the knee of his trouser-leg and discarded it.

'I understand that you visited a Mr Marcus Poole yesterday morning.'

'That's right,' agreed Raven. He had made no mystery about his visit. Poole had taken his visiting card. Poole must have complained to the police.

Manning's eyes were still roving the room. They settled on the passage that ran to the kitchen and bedrooms. Then his gaze came back to Page.

'Any objection to telling me why you're here, Mr Page?'

It was Raven who answered. 'He's here on a personal matter.'

Manning digested the answer thoughtfully. 'What kind of personal matter?'

Raven was getting impatient. 'One that he isn't prepared to discuss.'

The detective superintendent arranged the corners of his mouth in a tighter pattern.

'How about last night,' he said, looking at Raven. 'Can you remember where you were between eight o'clock and ten?'

Raven had no difficulty in answering. 'I was sitting right here in this room,' he said. He pointed a finger at Page. 'With him.'

Manning wheezed a chuckle. 'A quiet evening on the river. Sometimes it pays to have neighbours.'

Raven tapped the end of a Gitane and lit it. 'Maybe I should tell you something before we go any further. I used to be in the force myself.'

'I know,' Manning said. 'John Raven, born in Spalding, Lincolnshire, eleventh of August nineteen forty-eight. Left Harrow College at the age of eighteen and joined the police.'

Raven blew smoke at the ceiling. 'We say Harrow School. Otherwise the rest of it's accurate.'

There was no change in Manning's tone. He spoke with the same faint mockery. 'Marcus Poole was murdered last night.'

Raven positioned his cigarette in the ashtray.

'His body was found shot through the head at close range. It shows all the signs of a professional killing.'

Alarms rang inside Raven's head. He chose his words carefully. 'Let me get something straight. Are you suggesting that I've got something to do with this murder?'

Manning raised a hand to fend off the suggestion. 'Did I say that?' he demanded righteously. 'Good God, no! Let's get some proper light on the matter. Murder's a job for the heavies. I'm only concerned with fraud. But Marcus Poole *did* work for Consol Electric and you *did* see him yesterday. All I'm trying to do is put matters in proper perspective.'

He turned towards Page, appealing to reason. 'And don't you get me wrong either. This isn't a reflection on you. I didn't even know you were going to be here.'

'This is harassment,' said Page, his face stiff with hostility. 'I signed the book at Chelsea police station just after six last night. Then I called Mr Raven and arranged to drop by. I left the boat at eleven.'

'No problem,' Manning said appeasingly. 'You know how it is, get a bee in your bonnet and so on.' He wiped his palms on his knees and pushed himself up. 'Well, I'll say good night.' He continued to stare at Page.

'One wrong move. One wrong move,' he said heavily. 'A whisper of evidence and your bail's revoked.'

Raven opened the door to the deck.

'Thanks for your co-operation,' said Manning. 'You may be getting a visit from other officers.'

'They know where to find me,' said Raven. He closed the door firmly.

The two men looked at one another. 'He wasn't joking,' said Raven.

'So what?' Page demanded. 'It's got nothing to do with me.' His face reddened suddenly. 'Hang on! You're not thinking that I've got something to do with Poole's death?'

Raven grinned, taking the edge off his words. 'You certainly had enough motive. No, I don't think you're involved, Philip. It looks as though I'm the one who's going to have to answer the questions. I've got to think of a plausible reason for being in Poole's place.'

Manning's visit seemed to have drained Page's energy. 'Henry Vyner's bringing Drusilla to see me later tonight. I'd like you to be there.'

Raven was closing a chink in the curtains. 'Why?'

'Moral support,' shrugged Page. 'I don't know, Drusilla seems closer to Henry than she is to me at the moment. It would make things easier if you were there.'

Raven swung round. 'What sort of time?'

'About seven?'

'I'll be there,' Raven promised.

Chapter Seven

Raven climbed the stairs to the second floor. A burnished brass plate identified his friend's office.

Patrick O'Callaghan
Solicitor & Commissioner for Oaths

Raven opened the door. Anne Pegwell looked up, stilling the machine-gun clatter of the electronic typewriter. She took off her headphones.

'Is he in?' Raven asked.

She nodded across the room. 'Like a bear with a sore head.'

She was a slim blonde, and forty-two years old. In Raven's judgement, she was the most reliable keeper of secrets in town. He opened the door to the lawyer's refuge. His friend was sitting behind a desk-top littered with documents. A leaf-extension to the desk carried a phone and an intercom system. A tailcoat and white piqué waistcoat hung on the back of the door. There was a photograph of O'Callaghan's parents standing on the steps of La Scala. Raven removed a pile of pink-taped briefs from a chair and sat down.

'Marcus Poole's dead,' he announced. 'Murdered.'

O'Callaghan flinched as though someone had struck him. 'Don't be ridiculous,' he said mechanically, pushing stray hair from his eyes. He was wearing his usual business attire, dark double-breasted suit and spotted bow tie.

'It's true,' said Raven. 'Page was on the boat with me when Manning turned up. He's the—'

'I know who he is, for God's sake!' the lawyer said fretfully.

Raven kept his voice calm. O'Callaghan was someone who usually managed to keep his temper. But if he lost his control the result could be disastrous.

'Manning wanted to know where I was between eight and ten last night.'

The lawyer groped through the papers in front of him until he found a bottle of aspirins. He swallowed two and groped for the coffee cup.

'I don't believe this!' he said, shaking his head.

'He tried to turn it into some kind of social visit,' said Raven. 'But the knives were out. It wasn't Page he was interested in, it was me. He knew exactly who I was. Someone had pulled my file.'

The telephone came to life under some papers. The lawyer ignored it.

'My God!' he said feelingly.

Raven nodded. 'Poole's death's got nothing to do with Page. That much I am sure of. Manning's found out that Poole was shot by a waiter who was delivering his supper. He used to get his food sent in from a restaurant in the neighbourhood.'

The phone had stopped ringing. O'Callaghan cleared his throat. 'You think Poole's death has something to do with the statement?'

'I'm sure of it,' Raven said soberly. 'One down and one to go, as they say.'

The lawyer blinked suspiciously. 'So? What's that supposed to mean?'

'I'd say you're next on the list,' replied Raven.

The colour drained from O'Callaghan's face. He leaned into the intercom. 'Don't put any more calls through, Anne.' He slumped back in his chair, staring at Raven. 'So what happens now?'

Raven spoke quietly. 'You've got to cancel whatever appointments you've got for the rest of the week. Then you get hold of Maureen and take the first plane to Paris. You can stay in our flat. I'll call the concierge and tell her you're coming.'

'I can't do that,' the lawyer protested. 'I'm due in Marylebone Magistrates' Court tomorrow morning. It's my duty day. There are all sorts of things that need doing. I can't just walk away from it all.'

Raven looked up from his fingernails. He was fast losing patience. 'In that case you'd better hire yourself a good bodyguard.'

The suggestion only alarmed his friend even more. 'What about Maureen? What can I possibly tell her?'

'Lies,' Raven said. 'The same as any normal person would do. You came to me asking for help, remember. You promised to do whatever I said. If you renege on the agreement I'm washing my hands of the whole affair. You take your chances without me.'

O'Callaghan bent over the intercom again. 'Will you please come in here, Anne?'

She stood in the doorway, notebook in hand. Raven took charge.

'Patrick wants you to call Marylebone Magistrates' Court and say that he's ill. Then call Air France and book a couple of seats on a flight to Paris tonight. Send someone to collect the tickets.'

The secretary suspended her jotting. She turned to the lawyer. 'You've got some heavy appointments tomorrow. Miss Rahvis for one.'

'Cancel it,' O'Callaghan said distractedly. 'I'm ill, Anne.' He looked across at Raven. 'When will I be back?'

'Who knows?' answered Raven. He smiled at the secretary. 'It won't be for long, Anne. I'm sure you can hold the fort.'

She took another quick glance at the lawyer. 'I'll get on with it right away,' she assured them. The door closed behind her.

'Kirstie's right,' said the lawyer. 'You have to turn everything into a drama.'

'I'll try to forget that you ever said that,' Raven replied. 'Where is Maureen now?'

'She's at home. What happens to Jamie?'

'He goes to the vet is what happens. Give me your house keys.' Raven pushed out his hand, palm uppermost.

O'Callaghan felt in his pocket and produced two keys. Raven took them. 'I need to get into your house if necessary. What you have to do now is get a good hold on yourself. Blame everything on me. You can hint that I'm involved in some scandal. That's why you're going to Paris. You need Maureen for moral support. She'll go for that, especially if I'm involved.'

'That's unfair,' said his friend. 'Maureen's very fond of you.'

The phrase put Raven in mind of his wife. It was one that she used to preface some damning remark.

'OK, now listen,' he said. 'As soon as you get to Paris go straight to the flat. And stay there until you hear from me. Don't phone me at home. In fact, don't phone anyone. Just wait until you hear from me.'

Anne Pegwell glanced up as O'Callaghan opened the door for Raven to leave.

'Your tickets are booked, Mr O'Callaghan. They're on their way over with a messenger. Your flight leaves from Heathrow at nineteen hours twenty.'

Raven smiled goodbye to her. He touched his friend's arm. 'We'll work this one out, Patrick,' he promised with total assurance.

Raven was already late for his meeting with Page. He walked carefully, avoiding icy patches between the mounds of snow. The death of Marcus Poole still worried him. It was hard to accept as coincidence. Henry Vyner's indigo blue Bentley was parked in front of the flat. The chauffeur made no acknowledgement as Raven walked by. Raven climbed the six steps and pressed the entry buzzer. The street door clicked open. The lift smelled of a scent that was unfamiliar to Raven. He followed it into Page's hallway. Page looked as though he had been drinking.

'Come on in, John,' he said expansively and led the way into the sitting room.

'You know Henry Vyner, of course?'

'Hello,' Vyner said pleasantly. Whatever Page might have told him about his truce with Raven seemed to have been accepted. Vyner was wedged in a spindle-backed chair, his plump arms resting on the side-bars.

'And this is my daughter Drusilla,' said Page. 'This is Mr Raven, darling.'

Drusilla Page rose to her feet. She was almost as tall as her father with paler red hair growing down to her shoulders. Lipstick and eyeliner had been discreetly applied. Her eyes were the colour of mint. She was wearing a white silk shirt with a black skirt that finished a few inches above her knees. Her flat shoes had buckles. Her smile was guarded.

'How do you do, Mr Raven?'

The scent Raven had noticed came from her. She wore no jewellery except a pair of turquoise earrings and a fun-watch with a plastic strap.

She resumed her seat gracefully, her eyes sizing up Raven.

Page twirled the half-empty bottle in the ice-bucket. 'A glass of champagne?'

'That'll be fine,' Raven said. He carried his drink to a seat on the couch. Page was sitting next to his daughter, opposite. She moved away very slightly as her father refilled his glass. Her own wine was untouched.

Her voice was well-modulated. 'Did you know my mother, Mr Raven?'

'I'm afraid not,' Raven said awkwardly. He was anxious not to say the wrong thing.

'Mr Raven's a new friend,' Page explained. 'He's helping me out.'

She ran her finger round the rim of her glass, still looking at Raven.

'What do you do?' she asked suddenly.

The question took him by total surprise. 'Me? I don't do anything, really.'

'He's retired,' said her father. He managed to catch his hiccup in time.

Henry Vyner stirred majestically. 'Mr Raven was a famous detective at New Scotland Yard.'

Drusilla's smile was polite. 'Really? You mean something to do with the Fraud Squad?'

Vyner's chuckle came from the depths of his ample stomach. 'Everything else but the Fraud Squad. Mr Raven was what the Americans call a maverick. The Metropolitan Police Force never succeeded in putting their brand on him.'

'But you *are* helping my father?' she persisted.

Raven moved on the couch. 'I'm doing whatever I can. I'm not sure how much help that will be.' It was weird how his involvement seemed to have dropped into place.

Frown lines dragged at Drusilla's forehead. 'Do you think my father will go to prison, Mr Raven?'

'I certainly hope not,' Raven answered.

Vyner's folded hands rose and fell on his stomach. 'I was sorry to hear about Marcus Poole.' The remark seemed addressed to no one in particular, a contribution to the general conversation.

Page made a chopping motion with the side of his hand. The gesture overturned the ice-bucket. Page managed to save it from falling.

'We're not here to talk about Marcus Poole,' he burst out. 'I had nothing good to say about him when he was alive. I haven't changed my opinion.'

He took the handkerchief Vyner was offering and wiped his wet sleeve. The tirade continued. Only the culprit had changed.

'We all know what my problem is,' he said, focusing on

his daughter. 'I've been dumped by everyone, including you, Drusilla. How do you suppose it feels, knowing that you blame me for your mother's death, that you'd really like to see me in jail?'

The outburst made Raven uncomfortable. Was this Page's idea of a heart-to-heart with his daughter?

'Do you really want to talk like this in front of a stranger, Papa?' said Drusilla.

'I think I'd better leave,' Raven said quickly.

Page was still shouting. 'You stay where you are! You're here at my invitation. There are things that have to be said and I want you to hear them.'

Drusilla wiped the corners of her mouth with a handkerchief. 'Very well, if that's what you really prefer. In the first place I do *not* want you to go to prison. You're my father. But this much is equally true. If it hadn't been for the way you treated us, Mamma would still be alive.'

Her voice held a bitter acceptance of what she believed to be true. Her father struggled for self-control.

'OK,' he said. 'Let's talk about what really happened. I did my best to keep you out of the Consol Electric mess. It was drink that destroyed your mother, not me.'

Drusilla took a cigarette from her bag. Raven leaned across and gave her a light. It worried him to see the hurt in her eyes.

'You live in a world of your own,' she told her father. 'You always have, ever since I can remember. You have no real thought for anyone else. No consideration. That's what it is, total selfishness. We'd have been penniless if it hadn't been for Uncle Henry. He footed the bills then, and he's still doing it.'

She ground out her barely smoked cigarette and looked at Raven. 'I'm sorry, I really am. You shouldn't have to listen to this.'

'Maybe I don't have the right, but let me ask you a question,' he said. 'Do you love your father?'

88

It took some time for her to answer, and then in a very small voice.

'Yes, I do.'

Vyner broke in. 'There's no question about Drusilla's feeling for her father. She was still at school when he left the country. It wasn't easy for a girl of that age to understand what was happening.'

'You're wrong,' she said. 'I understood only too well. That was the problem.'

She brushed the ash from her lap, took her glass into the kitchen and kissed Page on the cheek.

'I have to go,' she said quietly. She trailed her hand across Vyner's cheek. ' 'bye, Uncle Henry.'

'I'm sorry, darling,' said Page. 'I really am.'

'Don't be,' she answered. 'It's just going to take time.'

Vyner helped her on with her coat. 'I'll come downstairs with you. The man can drive you home.'

She collected her handbag from the couch, straightened a cushion. She seemed calm and in command of the situation.

'You're a kind person,' she said, looking at Raven. 'Do you think I could come and see you some time?'

'Why not?' he said, widening his arms. 'Your father has my address and you know my wife.'

'Your wife?' she repeated.

'We gave Mrs Raven a lift home from Canada House, remember?' said Vyner.

The memory grew in her eyes. 'Of course! Then I definitely *will* come and see you,' she promised.

Her scent lingered after she had left the room with Vyner. Raven's voice was casual.

'How did Vyner know that Poole was dead?'

Page looked surprised. 'I spoke to him after I'd been to see you.'

Raven stopped at the window, watching the Bentley being driven away. Vyner was back in a couple of minutes. He looked across in Page's direction, shaking his ponderous head.

'When are you going to learn, Philip?'

'Forget it,' said Page. 'I'm in no mood for a lecture.'

There was the same suggestion of challenge between them that Raven had sensed before. A hint of competition for the girl's affection.

'You're a fool,' said Vyner. 'Drusilla's never stopped loving you. It's her respect that you have to earn. Anyway, I am glad that she left when she did. I wanted to talk about Loeb.' He sat down, his bulk expanding visibly. 'I saw him this afternoon. They're supposed to be getting copies of the prosecution evidence. They still don't know who made the statement.'

Raven looked up from his nails. 'The name'll be changed by the time the trial comes round. It's what's said that matters, not the name of the person who said it. Had Loeb heard that Marcus Poole was dead?'

Vyner's extra chins wobbled. 'If he did he didn't mention it. He gives me an odd feeling. He has this reputation for telling his clients what they want to hear.'

'How much are these people getting?' Page demanded.

'They've had twelve thousand pounds to date,' Vyner said. 'Most of that goes to Horobin. That's not the total bill, of course. Just retainers.'

Page hit his forehead with the thick part of his palm. 'Whichever way I turn, I'm still faced with this bloody statement.'

Vyner brooded for a couple of heavy-breathing minutes.

'Let's try to make sense,' he suggested. 'Let's see what we've got here.' He fixed on Page. 'There are two people you hold responsible, right?'

'That's right,' replied Page.

'And now one of them's dead, which leaves Raven's friend. Where's he at the moment?'

'He's out of town for a few days,' said Raven. 'But he's not our man, you can bank on it.'

Vyner's plump fingers were drumming his thighs. 'We've got to face facts. There are only two things that Philip can do. Stand trial or make a run for it. I think he should run.'

'Run where?' Page asked sourly.

'Get out of the country and play for time,' Vyner answered. 'Go somewhere safe where there's no extradition. Give things time to die a natural death.'

'A natural death?' Raven broke in. 'Have you any idea what you're talking about? The man's out on five hundred thousand pounds bail. *Half a million*! That's how much you lose if he doesn't show up for his trial. And don't forget that the police have his passport.'

'The money isn't important,' said Vyner. 'What matters is Philip's future. My own feeling is that he won't have a chance if he does turn up. We'll have to find some way of getting him out of the country.'

Page's face reddened under the sun tan. 'This is great! You people are sitting here, banging on about what I should do. Let *me* make the decisions! What about changing lawyers?'

'Waste of time, and money,' said Raven. 'Added to which you've got the best in the business. But you're right. The decision has to be yours.'

Vyner looked at his watch and walked to the window. The Bentley had not returned. Raven rose to his feet.

'I have to go,' he told Page. 'I'll talk to you later.'

Page came to the lift with him. 'I made you a promise,' said Raven. 'You owe me the chance to fulfil it.' The lift stopped and the gate slid back. 'Think about it!' he warned.

Raven went out to the street. The Bentley had still not returned.

Raven turned up his coat collar and started walking. The cold seemed to have isolated the flotilla of boats even more. Black water stretched into the darkness, its surface reflecting the lights from the houseboats. Raven turned right on to Old Church Street. Patrick O'Callaghan's home was wedged between a picture gallery and an estate agent.

Wrought iron enclosed a flagged forecourt half the size of a tennis-court. The car was missing. The two-storey house was painted yellow outside with a white entrance and window frames. Raven knew it well. There were three bedrooms, drawing room and a dining room next to the kitchen. Lights were burning upstairs and over the front door. A time-switch controlled them. Any attempt at unauthorised entry triggered an alarm in Chelsea police station.

Raven let himself in with O'Callaghan's keys. A life-size statue of Saint Francis of Assisi dominated the hallway, a relic from an abandoned church in Tuscany. The passage of time had dulled paint and chipped corners. He turned off the burglar alarm and walked through to the drawing room. Paisley-edged calico curtains hung in the windows. The room still smelled of cigar smoke. It was a comfortable, lived-in room with a gilt-framed mirror hanging over the fireplace. Chrysanthemums bloomed in the empty grate. Oversized cushions dotted the floor. The walls were decorated with ballet prints. A chewed rubber bone lay in the dog-basket.

Raven opened a cupboard. The champagne had left him thirsty. He poured lime juice into a glass and added Perrier water. There was no ice. He stretched out his legs in an armchair. He had little idea what he was doing there. There was a vague hope that whoever had killed Poole would come after O'Callaghan. The event was unlikely but he could not afford to ignore it.

He sipped his drink, thinking back on the scene he had just left. Page and the girl had his sympathy. And as far as Raven could see, Vyner's assessment was accurate. More than anything else, Drusilla and her father had to learn to respect one another. It was Vyner's suggestion that Page should abscond that Raven found strange. The loss of the bail bond didn't matter. Vyner was rich. The only answer was that Vyner was simply repeating what the lawyer had said.

Raven lit a cigarette. No one seemed to accept the fact that Poole still could have made the statement. If so, Page had to be off the hook, surely. Could an affidavit made by a dead man have any force in law? The alternative was that Poole's death was a coincidence. Raven set small store in fortuitous happenings. Instinct told him that Page was not lying. The thought of O'Callaghan as a killer was absurd. The question of motive was all-important.

The telephone came to life on the side table, its shrill insistence disturbing the peace of the house. Raven made no attempt to pick up the instrument, choosing to wait until the answering machine took over. When the call came to an end Raven ran the tape back. The caller spoke in a hurry.

'The person you asked about was shot dead last night. I'll let you know when and if I hear more.'

Raven erased the tape. It was no time for a message like that to be found. He lifted the phone and dialled Paris. The O'Callaghans should be there by now. The lawyer's voice sounded cautious.

'I'm at your place,' said Raven. 'Someone's just left a message on your answering machine, talking about Poole being shot. What the hell do you think you're playing at?'

'It was a friend,' said O'Callaghan. 'Someone who knows Marcus Poole.'

'Let me talk to Maureen,' said Raven. Maureen O'Callaghan came on the line.

'Look, I'm really sorry,' said Raven. 'I wouldn't have put you through all this if there'd been an alternative. I've got myself in a bit of a jam. Patrick's doing his best to help me out of it. I'm sorry, Maureen.'

She tinkled a laugh. 'I suppose I'll be told when the moment is right. You know how he loves being mysterious.'

'It shouldn't take long,' he said. 'I promise to make it up to you. Why don't you buy yourself something to wear and send me the bill?'

'Music to my ears,' she said. 'In the mean time there's lots of good food and the flat is beautifully warm. If we're not back by Tuesday, pop into the vet's and have a quick word with Jamie. The vet's got him upstairs with his children.'

'I'll do that,' he promised. 'And thanks for being so understanding.'

He replaced the phone and sat, waiting for something to happen. It was half past ten when he reactivated the burglar alarm and locked up the house. He was a hundred yards past the boats when he saw the car drawn up in front of Embankment Gardens. Raven continued to walk. A figure emerged from the back of the car as Raven approached the steps. It was Detective Superintendent Manning with his nondescript clothes and scoutmaster's cheerfulness.

'I've been waiting,' said Manning. 'You won't mind if I come up with you?'

Raven paused with his hand on the buzzer. 'Page may not like it.'

Manning closed his right eye. 'Why don't you ask him?'

'It's me,' Raven said into the entryphone. 'I've got Manning down here with me.'

'Nice company you keep,' replied Page. 'Come on up.'

Page was waiting in the doorway of the flat. The three men walked through to the sitting room. Raven sat down on a chair near the window.

Page closed the door to the hallway. 'You don't give up, do you?' he said, looking at Manning.

The detective superintendent waved a hand. 'All in the line of duty. Is anyone else here?' He glanced towards the bedroom.

'No one,' said Page, shaking his head. 'Who did you expect to find?'

Manning lowered himself on to the couch, holding his burned trilby in his lap.

'Does the name Paolo Rossi mean anything to you?'

'Nothing,' said Page. His eyes found Raven.

'Me neither,' said Raven.

Manning removed his hat. 'He's the man who killed Marcus Poole.'

'I didn't know the Fraud Squad dealt with murder,' said Raven.

'They don't,' Manning said comfortably. 'Things are done

differently since your day. There's more *esprit de corps*. People exchange information. You sit there scratching your balls and suddenly the phone goes. It turns out that we've got a real live informer.' He was releasing each piece of information like a conjuror performing his tricks.

'I never had dealings with informers,' said Raven.

Manning winked again. 'This one knows the game. I heard the tape. He sounded as though he'd got a lemon in his mouth. There was no time to have the call traced. He said if the police went to this carpark in Shepherd's Bush we'd find the man who killed Poole. We found him all right, with the front of his face blown away.'

Raven said nothing. In spite of what Manning had said, the police clearly suspected a link between Page and Poole's death.

'It's good of you to come here and tell us the news,' Page said ironically.

Manning dredged a crumpled piece of newspaper from his pocket. He spread it out on the table, front page showing.

'You've seen this, of course?' he asked Page.

Page considered the picture. It showed him getting off the 747 at Heathrow.

'I've seen it,' he said. 'What about it?'

Manning refolded the newspaper and dropped it back in his overcoat pocket. 'This copy's special,' he said. 'It was found in the car that Rossi was driving.'

The flat was suddenly quiet. Raven broke the silence.

'What the hell's that supposed to mean?'

Manning paid no attention to him. 'They took Rossi's prints. This was faxed through from Interpol just a couple of hours ago.' He dipped into his pocket again. This time it was a flimsy piece of copy-paper. Page read it over Raven's shoulder. The text was in English.

INTERPOL ROMA
Subject Rossi, Paolo. Born Bolzano 4/5/62. Studied at

Rome University. Disappeared from Italy following investigations into murdered Judge Clemente Minelli. International warrant for subject's arrest circulated members Interpol, 7/8/80. Warrant is still in force. Subject's last known address Ajax Hotel Amsterdam. Subject has no known associates. Extreme caution advised in subject's arrest or detention. Inform Ministry of Justice if apprehended.

Raven returned the printout. 'Do they know that he's dead?'

'They do now,' said Manning.

Raven was aware of the tightness in Page's face. Nervousness would be natural enough in the circumstances.

Raven scratched through his hair, locating an itch in his scalp. 'For a man with those sort of notices, Rossi doesn't seem to have been that smart. How did you find out where he was living?'

Manning, too, seemed aware of Page's nervousness. 'He had the key to his room in his pocket. He'd removed the tag but the key was a Banham. There was a number stamped on the shank. That took us straight to Draycott Place. Room number thirteen, would you believe! There was another key hidden under the bed. Rossi'd left his passport and a large sum of money in a locker at Victoria Station.' He popped his cheeks a couple of times, looking from Raven to Page. 'There's one thing that still bothers me.'

'What's that?' Page asked from the window.

Manning looked pleased with himself. 'Whoever killed Rossi did us a favour. I want to know who hired Rossi.'

'The same person who killed him,' said Raven. He yawned pointedly. 'And that's what you've been hanging around in the cold for – waiting to put our minds at rest?'

'No,' said the superintendent. 'The fact is I came here to ask a favour.'

'Not from me,' Raven said quickly. 'I wouldn't give a cop

the time of the day. He'd probably claim that the watch was stolen.'

Manning nodded. 'You've caused a lot of trouble in your time. Good men have gone to jail because of you. Some are still there, men with families, paying for one mistake. You won't get the chance to do the same thing to me. That much I'm sure about.'

Raven managed to control his feelings. 'You still haven't said what this favour is.'

Manning's voice was precise and stripped of its false geniality. 'There's a body on a slab in the mortuary. I think it has something to do with the charge that your friend here is facing. I know who this man is, where he stayed here in London. I'd like you to take a look at the corpse. There's a chance that you might have seen him somewhere.'

Raven looked at him with open contempt. 'I'm not sure what game it is that you think you're playing. You're giving me a hard time over something we don't know the first thing about. And you have the gall to come here and ask us to look at a man with only half a face left! You're not only stupid, you're totally charmless. If this were my flat I know what I'd tell you to do.'

Page came to life suddenly. He threw the front door open. 'Out!' he ordered, jerking his thumb.

Manning took his time, buttoning his overcoat and adjusting his scarf. He walked to the lift and turned back. 'You've just made a big mistake,' he warned.

'I'm doing it all the time,' Page replied. He shut the front door and looked at Raven. 'Don't even bother saying it. I've never even heard of Paolo Rossi.'

Raven dropped the curtain. Manning was climbing into the car below.

'He's gone,' he said.

'Good riddance,' said Page. He stared at the spot where Manning had been sitting. 'That bastard's been on my back ever since I arrived at Heathrow. Shouldn't I be able to do something about it? Get Loeb to complain or something?'

'A waste of time,' Raven said. 'Manning could say that he's doing his job. There's always the chance that one of us might have recognised Rossi. Manning's got nothing to lose in trying.'

Page was walking, stopping and walking again. 'I've got to do something,' he said desperately. 'I'm in court in a couple of days.'

'When are you going to be committed for trial?' Raven asked.

Page hunched his shoulders. 'They didn't say. Horobin's trying to get the case listed for the Old Bailey next month.' He turned his head quickly. Red stubble was pushing through his sun tan. 'I don't know what to do any more.'

'We've got two days at least,' Raven answered. 'That's time enough for you to make up your mind.'

'About what?' Page said cautiously.

'Skipping the country,' said Raven.

'Suppose I did,' ventured Page. 'What would happen?'

'There's no mystery about that,' Raven said. 'Your bail would be revoked and the magistrate would issue a warrant for your arrest. They'd have your picture up on the screens within minutes at every port in the country.'

Page brooded for a moment. 'Suppose I do make a run for it, what would I use for a passport? Could you help?'

'No,' Raven said shortly. 'The deal we made doesn't include false passports. Added to which they're not easy to get hold of these days.'

'How about these travel documents you get at the post office?'

'That's always possible,' Raven allowed. 'All it needs is some time spent in the registry office, checking on deaths of people roughly your own age. Then you find the guy's place and date of birth and use his particulars. That and a couple of photographs are all you need. But there's one problem. A British travel document is limited in scope. Only a few countries accept them.'

Page leaned his back against the wall. 'I'll have to think. What's your advice, John?'

'My advice?' Raven thought for a minute. 'There's a risk attached to whatever you do. You're the one who has to decide.'

Page changed the subject. 'What did you think of Drusilla?'

'I liked her,' Raven said frankly. 'Though I'm not quite sure what goes on in her head.'

Page came off the wall. 'That's part of the reason for asking you here tonight. It seems to have worked. She was more open-minded at least, and ready to talk.'

'She's young,' Raven said. 'And she's got the same worries that you have.'

'I've got to be sure how she feels before I make up my mind,' Page said. 'I mean how she'd react if I went on the run.'

'You've got a big problem there,' said Raven. 'The girl's still trying to come to terms with the fact that you're back in her life. I think she ought to be told about the trust fund. She should know where the money really comes from.'

'I can't do that,' said Page. 'It's too late. Added to which Henry's her Rock of Gibraltar. It would destroy her to know that he'd lied too.'

'But that's what he has done,' Raven said, smiling.

Page's expression and voice remained obstinate. 'Henry only did what I asked him to do. Look, you heard what Drusilla said. She doesn't want to see me in jail. OK, so why can't you sound her out, put the alternative to her?'

'That's nice,' Raven said. 'You want me to ask your daughter how she'd react if you were sitting in Rio with the rest of the troubled in spirit? That's if you ever managed to get as far as Brazil.'

Page's eyes stared from a worried face. 'Will you do it or not?'

A rush of sympathy stilled Raven's reluctance. 'I'll do it on one condition.'

'Name it.' Page's expression was serious.

'I want your word that you'll do nothing rash until I've had a little more time to think about the statement.'

Page covered his heart with his hand. 'You've got my word on it. Talking about the statement, what has happened to Patrick O'Callaghan?'

'You heard what I said to Manning. He's gone to the country until your trial's over. He thinks that he's starting a gastric ulcer.'

'Too bad,' said Page. 'We had some weird times together. It was a weird period in my life, come to think of it.'

Raven inspected his nails again. He wondered if he should go to his wife's manicurist. 'There's one thing you have to think about seriously,' he counselled. 'It's going to have a bearing on your relationship with your daughter. You have to decide whether or not you're guilty.'

'What's that supposed to mean?' Page said, his eyes narrowing.

Raven shook a Gitane from the pack. 'I'm not talking about legal guilt. I mean, how do you square yourself morally? That's the real issue as far as your daughter's concerned. I'm still not clear in my head about it. You took fourteen million pounds from Consol Electric. And you didn't deliver. Do you think that's morally right?'

Page dwelt on the question. 'Maybe not,' he said finally. 'But you could say the same thing about a hundred deals that go down every day in the City. What do you suggest I do? Return what's left of the money and beg for forgiveness? I'm just not going to do that, John.'

'I was talking about Drusilla,' said Raven. 'And respect.'

Page consulted his watch. 'When can you see her?' He was about to pick up the phone.

'Hold it!' said Raven. 'Are you sure that you want me to

go through with this? Why don't you just sit down and talk, the pair of you?'

'Because of what she might say,' Page replied. 'I can't bear the thought of losing her.'

Raven nodded. Maybe that's how it was with parents and children, an entirely different set of needs and values. God knew, he was no expert. 'I'll see her any time,' he said. 'When does she finish work?'

Page had the phone in his hand. 'I'm not sure if it's five or six. It doesn't matter. She's a pupil. She can leave any time. Can she come to the boat?'

'Why not? I'll be glad of the company. If six is all right I'll make sure I'm there.'

Page dialled. 'It's me, darling! Were you sleeping? No, good. Listen, Mr Raven would like to have a word with you tomorrow evening. Round about six. He's invited you on to his boat. It's moored at the bottom of Oakley Street. It's called the *Albatross* and it's painted white. OK?'

'I know where it is,' Drusilla replied. 'We gave his wife a lift home one night. What does he want to see me about?'

Page rolled his eyes at the ceiling. 'Because you asked him if you could visit him. Or don't you remember?'

'I'll be there at six,' she promised.

Page put the phone down. 'She'll be there.'

Raven yawned and rose to his feet. 'I need some sleep. Good night.'

It was still cold outside. Raven sank his neck deep in his upturned collar. The snow-heavy clouds had lifted, leaving a pale sliver of moon over Battersea Park. Ice crunched underfoot as he descended the steps to his boat. It was after midnight and most of his neighbours' homes were in darkness. He let himself into the peace of his sitting room.

He poured himself a nightcap to go with the sandwich he made and ate standing up in the kitchen. He took the drink to the bedroom and ran a bath. Clean pyjamas felt good against his skin. He turned off all the lights except the lamp on the bedside table. He lay back on the pillows, glass in one hand and called Canada.

'That does it,' his wife said tartly. 'That makes four times in a week you've called me. You must have a guilty conscience.'

He tipped on his side, compensating for the roll of the barge.

'It's a wicked world,' he said amiably. 'But it leaves me untouched. I just wanted to hear your voice. That girl I was talking about, the one who gave you a lift back from Canada House. I'm entertaining her tomorrow night.'

'Really?' Her voice was as brittle as glass.

'I thought you should know,' he said.

'Well, keep your clothes on,' she advised. 'You're not a pretty sight without them. Anyway, isn't she the girl whose father stole all that money?'

'That's what they say,' he replied.

'What on earth are you doing with her?'

'She needs advice. Look, what I'm really calling to say is that Patrick and Maureen are using Ile St Louis for a few days. Patrick's got business in Paris.'

'Know something?' she said. 'You're the most infuriating man I ever met. Talk about lateral thinking. Your mind has to go sideways.'

He held the receiver away from his ear until she had finished.

'How's your leg?' she asked finally.

'I'm thinking of having it off,' he replied. 'Varicose veins, hair falling out. The next thing's a mouthful of National Health teeth. You're talking to a broken man. Bye-bye.' He smacked a couple of kisses into the mouthpiece. Then he finished his drink, turned out the bedside lamp and was asleep within minutes.

At nine o'clock the next morning Raven took a cab straight to the Royal Automobile Club. He made a collection of the day's newspapers and took them downstairs. There was only one other man having breakfast. He read through the newspapers diligently, drinking numerous cups of coffee. The only mention of a body being found in a Shepherd's Bush carpark was a paragraph in *Today*. The details were sparse. The victim had been shot by an unknown assailant. No names were disclosed. An investigation was under way.

At ten thirty Raven called the accountant at his bank. He asked for a credit check to be run on Henry Vyner. He told them where he was. The man promised to get back to him. The return call came in half an hour. The accountant told Raven that Henry Vyner's standing was impeccable. Did Raven want the details to be sent by post? Raven said no. He swam a few lengths in the pool and had a massage. It was after three when he left the RAC and walked up to Piccadilly. Fortnum and Mason was crowded with pre-Christmas shoppers. Raven bought a large bunch of freesias, two hundred and fifty grammes of Beluga caviare and a selection of canapés. The more Page relied on him, the deeper Raven's sympathy grew. The trap was familiar. The old fox was back on the trail with his nose to the ground.

A cab dropped him back at the boat. He glanced across at the cul-de-sac. High walls prevented the sun from reaching the ground between. His car was still there. The houseboat was spotless. Mrs Burrows had left a note. The newspaper shop had called. Raven had forgotten to pay their bill. He scribbled a cheque and put it in an envelope. He transferred the canapés and caviare to the refrigerator. The freesias he put in a cut-crystal vase that Kirstie had found in Prague. The warm room brought out their fragrance.

Five o'clock. It was getting darker outside by the minute. He selected tapes to play as background music. Bach, a few Brazilian cassettes and Bob Marley's 'Exodus.' He changed his clothes wryly, remembering his wife's remark about his body. Conceit died hard, he reflected. But there was no harm in indulging it now and again. He chose his brass-buttoned blazer, grey flannel trousers and plain black loafers. Five thirty. He switched on the overhead light at the top of the steps and opened the drinks cupboard. He set a silver tray with Scotch, sherry and a bottle of chilled Blanquette. He added orange juice as an afterthought.

The Tiffany standard lamp diffused soft light the length of the sitting room. A Bach fugue was playing when the door buzzer sounded. Raven released the catch and stood in the open doorway.

Drusilla came in from the cold, wearing a tailored coat over black skirt and white blouse. Her pale-red hair was tied at the back of her neck. Raven took her coat and closed the door.

She stopped still in front of his painting, moving her head from side to side. 'This is the first Klee I've ever seen outside a museum or gallery. Where did you get it?'

Raven hung her coat in the corridor cupboard. 'I laid out a thousand pounds for it twenty-four years ago.'

Her mouth turned down. 'I suppose you know what it's worth today?'

'I prefer not to think,' he said. 'The insurance premiums are crippling. What can I get you to drink? If you don't see what you want, I've probably got it somewhere.'

She had the fine skin of a redhead with frown marks at the sides of her eyes. She contemplated the array of bottles on the tray. 'May I have vodka and orange juice?'

He fixed her drink and carried his own Scotch and water to the seat on the couch next to her. He lifted his glass in her direction.

'Welcome aboard.'

She smiled, her eyes fixed on Kirstie Raven's photograph.

'Your wife's very beautiful,' she said quietly. She put a blob of caviare on a finger of toast and swallowed it. 'You're a weird man, Mr Raven. I don't mean weird-weird, just strange. You don't really know my father and yet you're doing all this stuff for him. Why?'

She was wearing the scent he remembered. He leaned

slightly forward. 'What is that you're wearing, I mean the scent?'

The question seemed to take her by surprise. 'It's called Ténéré by Paco Rabanne. Do you like it?'

He nodded. 'About your father,' he said. 'He wasn't the reason originally. I got involved through someone else, a friend.' He reached for the jar of caviare. 'I suppose you know why we're here?'

'You mean now?' She made a face. 'Do I get Brownie points for guessing correctly?'

He took a slug of his Scotch. 'It's to do with your father, Drusilla. I imagine you know about this statement that's been made against him.'

Her head rose and fell. 'Uncle Henry told me about it. I'm still not clear in my head what it means.'

'It's an exceptionally damning piece of evidence. If the prosecution use it there's a strong possibility that your father will go to jail. And there's no chance they won't use it.'

She poked at the ice in her glass with a forefinger. Her nails were well kept, the varnish clear. She looked up. 'There's something I don't understand, Mr Raven.'

He held up a hand. 'John. If we're going to be friends. What don't you understand?'

'No one seems to know who made this statement. How can they use it against my father? I thought everyone had the right to face his accuser.'

'There are exceptions,' said Raven. 'And I'm afraid this is one of them.'

'I love this river,' she said suddenly. 'I can almost see your boat from my bedroom window.'

He pushed the caviare across the table in front of them. 'Eat up!' he instructed. 'This stuff never tastes the same once the air has got to it.'

She scooped up the glistening roe and squeezed lemon juice over it. She wiped her fingers on the edge of her napkin.

'I never even thought about people in prison before. I

mean, I've seen films and TV, of course. But that was just make-believe. That's all changed now. There can't be anything worse than losing your freedom.'

The fugue had come to an end. Raven put on Bob Marley and turned down the volume.

Drusilla seemed fascinated by Kirstie's photograph. She took the frame in her hands and read the inscription.

'"May the love last as long as the bone structure!" What a romantic thought. You must miss her?'

'She'll be back in a couple of weeks,' he said carelessly. 'Thank God,' he added, prompted by a feeling of guilt.

She pulled a hand-mirror from her bag and inspected her eyeliner.

'Your wife said that you've got a flat in Paris?'

The remark made Raven cautious. It was an innocent question but one that was too close to O'Callaghan for comfort.

'That's right,' he said. 'It belonged to Kirstie's brother. He died. We don't use it that often.'

She took the cigarette and light that he offered her.

'If my father's found guilty, how long will he get?'

'How long?' he hedged. 'Well, there's a lot of money involved.'

'How long?' she insisted.

'It could be as much as ten years,' he said quietly.

'Ten years!' Her voice was shocked. She sat down again and leaned forward, her shoulders heaving. She started to weep.

He drew her head up. Her cheeks were streaked with mascara. He wiped her eyes with her napkin. She attempted a smile.

'I'm sorry,' she sniffed.

'There's no need to be,' he replied. 'He's your father.' Her cigarette had burned out in the ashtray. He lit another and gave it to her.

'He'll kill himself,' she said with sudden conviction. 'I'm sure of it. You must know what goes on in those places, the squalid indignities. The hopelessness of it all. He would never be able to take it.' She drank a token sip from her glass and then put it down again. 'What are we going to do?' she whispered.

He chose his words carefully. 'He could abscond. Just get on a plane and keep going.'

Her eyes sought his hopefully. 'But the police have his passport.'

'Let's just suppose it were possible,' he argued. 'How would you feel?'

'Feel?' she repeated. 'You're offering me the choice between my father dead or alive. I want him alive. I love him.'

There was no more talk of respect and Raven steered clear of it.

'Then why don't you tell him so?' Raven said. 'You're all he's got left.'

She looked at him closely. 'Is that the real reason you asked me here? To tell me that Papa is running away?'

'I didn't say that,' he answered. 'All I did was ask how you'd feel if he did run away.'

Her fingers strayed to an earring. 'Does Uncle Henry know about this?'

The couch sagged as he sat down beside her again. 'There's nothing to know up to now. In any case there's only so much that Vyner can do. Things have gone beyond his control.'

She looked up very slowly. 'You don't seem to understand. Uncle Vyner knew Mamma before my father did. It was Uncle Henry who introduced Mamma to him. As long as I can remember, Uncle Henry's always been there to help. He's been our Rock of Gibraltar.'

Raven spat out a prawn carcass. 'I know about that. No one could ask for a better friend. But there's only so much he can do, Drusilla. And that's about the long and short of the matter.'

Drusilla moved almost imperceptibly closer. 'Then who is there who can help?'

'You can,' he urged. 'Right now you're the most important person in your father's life.'

She stayed silent in thought for a while, then her mouth curved in a smile.

'I can remember once, Papa came down to school to see me. Mamma was in Austria. It wasn't my birthday and the nuns let him take me out for lunch. I was so proud, you know? Thirteen years old with my beautiful father. I wanted all my friends to see him. I remember him asking me what I wanted to be when I grew up. I had no idea. He told me what he wanted was for me to be happy. He said the best way to do that was to do what I wanted, as long as I wasn't deliberately hurting anyone else. It's something I always remember. What was your father like?'

'I never knew him,' said Raven. 'My parents were killed by a bomb during the war. I was two years old. My aunt brought me up.'

She was still caught in her own personal tragedy. 'I would never betray him, no matter what! I *do* love my father. I love him in spite of everything.'

She picked up her bag. 'I think I'd better go home now. Thank you for being so kind.'

He was moved by her obvious gratitude. He waited on deck until he heard the door slam at the bottom of the steps. Her footsteps clicked away hurriedly.

He stretched out on the couch. The hormones secreted were running into his bloodstream making the unlikely plausible. What he believed came from his street sense, a defiance of all probability. He knew that his hunch was right as though God's writ on the wall was in front of him. What he had to do now was prove it.

He picked up the phone. 'Drusilla's just left. We had a long talk. You couldn't have hoped for a better reaction. I wish I had a daughter like that.'

'Can I come round and see you?'

'Do that,' said Raven. He wanted Page to feel at home.

Most of all he wanted to read Page's eyes under pressure. The door buzzer sounded promptly. Page came into the room bundled into a brown leather jacket with a woollen collar. He removed the jacket and flopped down, tired and disconsolate.

Raven slid the tray in Page's direction. There were canapés left, half a pot of caviare. Page paid attention to neither.

'We talked for the best part of an hour,' Raven said. 'There's no question whose side she's on. She'll go along with whatever you decide to do. She made that very plain. You might as well know it – she doesn't think you'd be able to handle a long sentence. Come to that, nor do I.'

He poured a glass of wine for his guest, helped himself to more Scotch and water. He raised his glass in a token gesture.

'I saw Loeb this afternoon,' said Page. 'He said the same thing as Henry, basically. He gave me this.'

Raven took the typewritten sheet and read it.

QUEEN'S BENCH DIVISIONAL COURT
(LORD JUSTICE RICHARDS AND MR JUSTICE ARGENT)
3 MAY 1990

A statement made by a witness to the police about an offence is admissible instead of oral evidence at full committal proceedings under Section 23 (3)(b) of the Criminal Justice Act 1988 where the witness is in fear as a result of the circumstances of the offence. The fear need not arise from an incident occurring after the offence which had put the witness in such fear as to be unable to attend the proceedings. The decision whether to admit the statement is then a matter of the court's discretion under section 26.

The report was on Ruthrauf and Ryan's legal stationery. Page's glass was already empty. Raven refilled it.

'Does that mean what I think it does?' queried Page.

'It means that the prosecution don't even have to produce their witness,' said Raven. 'A charter for police informers.'

Page drew a long breath. 'You've been saying that all along. What matters in a statement is what's said, not who says it.'

Raven put the judgement in his desk. 'I'll keep this. OK. Let's get our brains working. This gives us two clear days before the hearing in the magistrates' court. You didn't tell Loeb you were thinking of running?'

Page shook his head, his eyes closed. He opened his eyes again. Raven stared into them.

Page's smile was ironic. 'Loeb says if it comes to the worst I'll be sent to an open prison. I'll be able to learn to speak Chinese or Russian. Both, for all I know. The bastard's got me inside already. I don't trust him.'

'So what have you decided to do?' asked Raven.

'Drusilla's twenty years old,' answered Page. 'Her whole life in front of her. The way things stand at the moment, her father's either going to be in jail or on the run for the rest of his life. That's not much of a prospect for her.'

'She thinks you'd kill yourself if they send you to prison,' Raven repeated.

'I just might do that,' said Page. 'It would solve a lot of problems.'

'Bullshit,' said Raven. Drusilla's voice was still in his memory. 'If you do decide to take off, I think she'll want to go with you.'

Page's face reddened. 'That's the last thing I need, for crissakes! Who the hell put that idea into her head?'

'It's what happens when people get confused,' said Raven. 'I've got an idea. I'm not going to say what it is at this moment. It's a desperate measure. But if it works, your troubles are over. Do you want to take a chance with me?'

'Why not?' said Page. 'I've been gambling for the last twenty years.' He was enjoying his wine now, not just drinking it.

Raven leaned forward. 'I said it's a desperate measure. It needs your total co-operation. Anything short of that and we're screwed.'

'Tell me,' said Page. The look in his eyes showed that his brain was working.

'That's the first rule,' said Raven. 'No questions. I need blind obedience. Without that the whole thing's a nonsense.'

'You've got a deal,' said Page, putting his hand out.

Raven hid his relief. This one was not just for Page but for Drusilla as well.

'Right, now listen. You're going to be on the BA flight to Madrid at twenty past nine tomorrow morning. They're an hour ahead. The plane arrives at twelve thirty, their time. An Iberia flight leaves Barajas for Havana, Cuba, at fourteen hundred hours. You'll be booked on it. Here are the details.'

He gave the paper to Page.

Page moved his head slowly. 'BA from Heathrow to Madrid, nine twenty tomorrow morning.'

'Not a word to Drusilla,' warned Raven. 'Henry will have to know of course, but it's important that he doesn't come to the airport. Make sure that he understands that.'

Page showed reluctance for the first time since their handshake. 'You know this just isn't making sense. Where's the passport going to come from?'

'Trust me,' urged Raven. 'Have you reported to the police station yet?'

'Over an hour ago. They've started making jokes about it.'

'Don't let that worry you,' Raven said with assurance. 'Go home and get a good night's rest. You're going to need it for tomorrow. And don't forget, not a word to anyone except Henry Vyner. OK?'

'OK,' said Page. He shrugged into his leather jacket. 'No wonder you left the police force. You must have been outrageous.'

Raven grinned. 'I was OK. People just didn't understand me.'

He opened the door to the deck. 'Be here at a quarter to eight in the morning. And trust me.'

'I will,' promised Page.

The door closed. For some reason the mention of trust left a feeling of embarrassment. Raven was unable to determine why. Alone in the sitting room, he picked up the phone again. He gave his name to a girl at BA reservations.

'I have the booking in front of me,' she said. 'Heathrow-Havana, Cuba, by way of Madrid. The fare is four hundred and seventy-eight pounds. And the ticket's in the name of Philip Page.' She checked the numbers on Raven's credit card. 'I'll issue the ticket, now, Mr Raven. I won't be on duty myself in the morning but the ticket will be here waiting for you. Have a good flight.'

He listened to the BBC news and read for an hour. The canapés and caviare had taken the edge off his appetite. He booked an alarm call for the following morning and dropped off to sleep, feeling pleased with himself.

Raven was sitting in the BMW. The motor had been running for several minutes and the interior of the car was comfortably warm.

It was ten minutes to eight on November the fourteenth. A grey sullen sky. The thermometer fastened to the mast of the boat gave a reading of 40° Fahrenheit. Raven had been dressed for an hour in a clean pair of cords, a J. Pressman button-down shirt and his lumberjacket. His suede shoes had thin soles. You never knew when a burst of speed might be needed. There were two packs of Gitanes on the dashboard and the day's newspapers on the back seat.

Heavy-duty trucks barrelled along the Embankment heading for the West Country and the Midlands. Reverse traffic carried the first influx of dormitory dwellers bound for the high-rise office blocks overlooking the eastern reaches of the river.

Philip Page came into sight, hurrying. He was wearing his shawl-collared leather jacket over a roll-necked sweater. He located the BMW and waited to trot through the traffic to where Raven was parked. Page slid into the seat beside Raven and stared across at the boats. Lights burned behind curtained windows. Men drank tea with one eye on the clock. Children were being fed and made ready for school. A spot of blood on Page's Adam's apple jumped as he spoke.

'I talked to Henry Vyner last night. He'd been trying to get hold of me for hours.'

'Did he say why?'

Page lifted his shoulders. 'He wanted to know what was happening.'

Raven looked right and left, waiting for a lull in the traffic. 'So you told him.'

'I told him.'

Raven engaged the gears, dropping in behind a 10-ton truck heading west. He could sense the defeat on Page's face without looking.

'What's the matter?' he challenged. 'Vyner didn't like the idea?'

'What he thought didn't come into it. All he asked was if I was sure I knew what I was doing. I said I'd made up my mind and that you were helping me.'

'So why the long face?'

'I don't know. I mean, this whole thing . . . '

Raven swerved the car to the verge and put his foot hard on the brakes. 'We've already been through all this. You want me to turn around and go back? If so, I'm telling you you'll be on your own.'

'I'm sorry,' said Page. His sun-tanned features were drawn.

'Did you sleep last night?' challenged Raven.

'On and off. I had plenty to think about. I'm out on bail,

driving to the airport to get on a plane with no passport. How
would you feel?'

Raven consulted the rear-view mirror. 'For one thing I'd
have more faith than you do.'

'I suppose you're right,' Page replied. 'It wasn't easy talking
to Henry. It wasn't so much what he said. I told him I couldn't
face the prospect of going to jail and he understood. He
promised he'd take care of Drusilla.'

A space appeared in the traffic. Raven pulled in again.
'Fasten your seat-belt,' he said quietly.

They drove in silence for the next four miles. Once on the
overpass, Raven moved into the fast lane. It was twenty past
eight, more than an hour before take-off. They were travelling
at sixty miles an hour on a flyover suspended high above the
ground, past multi-floored office buildings and factories. A
low precipitate of smog hung about the supports of the
understructure.

Page found his voice again. 'I told Henry not to come to
the airport. He wouldn't have done in any case. He said if
anything should go wrong they might get him for collusion.'

'Fair enough,' Raven agreed. 'Is that how you left things
with him?'

'Yes. He gave me a number to call when I get to Havana.'

'A Cuban number?'

'No, a number in London. That's where he'll be.' He was
holding a slip of paper in his hand.

A sign loomed in front of them. Raven swung the car left
on the northern perimeter road and into the echoing tunnel.
He drove into the short-stay carpark opposite Terminal One.
There was space on the first floor. He backed into a free slot
near the bridge across to the main building. He hooked the car
keys out of the ignition lock and dropped them in Page's lap.

'Hang on to these. You may have to drive the car back. If
that should happen, leave it in the usual place in the cul-de-sac
and go home. If I haven't called by five o'clock, make your
report at the police station.'

Page looked faraway for a second, remote. His laugh was short and on one note. 'When *am* I going to be able to ask some questions?'

Raven patted him on the knee. 'Sooner than you expect, with luck. What you have to do for the moment is concentrate your brain on what's happening. There's a pre-pay parking booth in the terminal. Buy a ticket so that you can get out fast if you have to.' He opened the glove compartment. 'Insurance and MOT certificates, log book.'

A car door slammed twenty yards away. A man came down the aisle carrying an overnight bag and walked on to the bridge.

Raven pulled the *Guide to Heathrow* from his pocket. He turned to a scale-drawn map of Terminal One.

'Pay attention,' he said, pointing down at the map.'The Main Hall's a hundred and fifty yards long by fifty. There are twelve check-in points lettered A to M. Most of them are manned by BA staff. There are other airlines as well. Those don't concern you.'

He placed the guide on the steering wheel and used a finger to trace place and position.

'You go up these stairs to the mezzanine. Walk as far as the buffet bar. You're up on the balcony now, looking right down at the main British Airways reservations desk. OK?'

Page nodded, leaning across Raven's shoulder.

Raven drew a line with his finger to a box marked International Departures and Passport Control.

'Hold on a minute,' said Page. 'What's going on here? What is all this? Who's leaving the bloody country – you or me?'

'Neither of us,' Raven answered. 'Just pay attention. All passengers go through here,' he tapped on the map again. 'All you'll see from the balcony will be a couple of guys sitting at desks. They're airport security. Their job's to make sure that anyone going through the barrier has a boarding card. Behind them is a screen. That's where the serious business starts. Passport Control. Is that clear?'

Years seemed to have dropped from Page's face. He was following Raven's every word and gesture.

Raven came back to the Reservations desk. 'This is where I collect the ticket. I walk fifty yards to the first control. You'll be able to see every move that I make. Your job's to keep your eyes on me for as long as you can. As soon as I'm out of sight go straight to the car and get the hell out of it. If you get stopped, you've come to meet a friend on a flight that arrived from Brussels at seven fifty-five. She didn't show up. You've been waiting to see if she's on a later plane. What's your friend's name?' he asked sharply.

Page answered without hesitation. 'Gabrielle Lazur.'

Raven smiled in spite of himself. 'Who the hell's she?'

'A French Canadian actress. A good one.'

'OK. I lent you my car. You give my name and address. If they ask where I am, you say you don't know. Don't worry, I'm just covering angles.'

Page straightened his back. 'You say neither of us is getting on the plane?'

'That's right,' Raven said. 'Do you ever pray?'

'Only when I'm in the shit,' answered Page.

'Make an exception,' said Raven. 'And say one for me.'

They crossed the bridge to Terminal One. Raven watched Page pre-pay for a couple of hours' parking time. Then Page climbed the stairs to the mezzanine and stationed himself on the balcony. Raven walked through the hall to the BA reservations desk. The adrenalin was surging now, sharpening his senses. His ears and eyes were on stalks. There were three girls and one man behind the counter. One of the girls was free. She greeted Raven, smiling welcome.

'Good morning, sir. How may I help you?'

He leaned on the counter, using what he hoped was charm. 'I'm supposed to be collecting a ticket, Heathrow-Madrid-Havana. The flight takes off at nine twenty.'

'And the name, sir?'

'Philip Page. The fare's already been paid.'

The ground hostess punched a few buttons and viewed the result on the screen at her side.

Raven sneaked a look at the balcony. Page was standing next to an Indian woman with children. Raven lit a cigarette.

'Here you are, sir,' the girl said. She gave Raven the ticket and boarding card. 'Check in over there,' she pointed.

Raven took his time in crossing the concourse, alive to the first hint of danger. He displayed his ticket and boarding card and walked towards the two immigration officers. Behind them was the paraphernalia of body and baggage checks. Moving belts, video screens and metal detectors. Raven chose the desk on the left. EEC PASSPORTS. Raven was holding the ticket and boarding card.

The officer was wearing dark glasses. He watched as Raven felt through his pockets, the smile on his face fading rapidly. Raven expressed first alarm then disbelief.

'This can't be true!' he said, shaking his head. 'Would you believe, I've forgotten my passport!'

The phone rang at the officer's elbow. He picked it up and listened. 'Take over, Jack,' he said to his colleague. Then to Raven, 'Will you please come this way, sir.'

He led Raven along a corridor, blocking any attempt Raven might make to make a run for it. Raven slowed his pace, seeking to maintain his composure. A man in an anorak came off the wall in front of them. He was carrying a walkie-talkie.

'In there,' said the immigration official, jerking his head at a half-open door. There were no windows in the room. The door had a spy hole. The walls were completely smooth. There was not one crack or crevice where as little as a cigarette-paper could be concealed. There was a metal chair and a formica-topped table. A copy of the regulations governing the illegal importation of drugs was sellotaped to a portable lavatory. There was no visible plumbing connection. Raven straddled the chair and fished for a cigarette. He was in one of the recovery units used to detain persons suspected of concealing contraband in their body cavities.

The door flew back suddenly. Detective Superintendent Manning stood with his hands pushed deep in the pockets of his shabby grey overcoat. The man in the anorak was a few yards down the corridor. Manning came forward behind a pointing finger.

'I should have known it was you. It had to be!'

Raven said nothing. He could hear the announcements over the tannoy. 'Scandinavia Airlines regret . . . Will the owner of the blue Ford Capri, registration number . . . This is the last call for passengers flying BA to Malta . . . '

He was being held in the Customs Zone between Passport Control and the runways.

Manning perched on the side of the table and grunted. 'I made a mistake about you. You're not only daft – you're dangerous. What the fuck do you think you're doing?'

He held up Raven's flight ticket and boarding card. Things were going the way Raven expected.

'Just making the moves, Superintendent. You know, playing the game.'

A vein thickened in the middle of Manning's forehead. 'I could nick you,' he snarled.

'On what charge?' Raven asked innocently.

Manning held up the ticket again. 'Since when is your name Philip Page?' The question only served to inflame the detective. 'Interfering with the course of justice,' he said. 'You've only got to cough to be guilty.'

It was important for Raven to talk his way out of trouble. He could not afford to spend time in a cell. Last calls for his flight had already been made. Page should be on his way back to the boat by now.

'Come on, now,' Raven said winningly. 'I bought a ticket in somebody else's name and I paid for it. I don't see the problem.'

'You don't see the problem,' Manning repeated scathingly.

'I've been up since six o'clock this morning. Two units busy flying round like farts in a colander. Airport security on red alert. And you don't see the problem!'

Raven raised his bony shoulders. 'I didn't make the phone call.'

Manning blinked and popped his cheeks. 'What phone call?'

'The one you had last night. The unidentified voice talking through a couple of pillows. A man. He told you that Philip Page was jumping bail. That he'd be on the plane for Madrid in the morning. It was impossible to trace the call, but you knew that the man was telling the truth.'

Manning threw the ticket and boarding card down on the table. 'Are you going to tell me what game you're playing?'

'It's a stalking horse,' Raven said. His fear of arrest was receding. Manning was genuinely puzzled. 'And it's worked,' Raven added.

Manning looked as though he had misheard. He took a cursory glance in the lavatory-bowl to see what Raven might have dropped there.

'A stalking-horse,' Raven repeated. 'It's something you hide behind when you're hunting.'

The detective superintendent was clearly out of his depth. He did his best to get back in control by use of sarcasm.

'How come Page flew BA through Madrid? He could have flown direct to Miami and hopped on the Miami shuttle. It would have been cheaper and quicker.'

'He must use the wrong travel agent,' said Raven.

The room was stifling, the thermostat set too high. Manning unbuttoned his overcoat. Memory made his expression sour. 'I've been up since six o'clock this morning. Is that what this is about, a stalking-horse?'

'It's about justice,' said Raven.

The word brought back the swollen vein between Manning's eyebrows. 'Justice? My job's got nothing to do with justice.

And nobody knows that better than you do. My job's nicking villains. Other people take care of justice.'

Manning threw the door wide. The noise brought the man in the anorak running.

'Get this man out of my sight,' Manning said.

'What do I charge him with?'

Manning's tone was dangerously reasonable. 'What's your name, officer?'

'DC Collins, sir.'

'And how's your hearing?'

The detective constable's expression was baffled. 'Fair to middling, sir.'

'Then open your bloody ears!' Manning roared. 'I said nothing about nicking him. I said get him out of my sight.'

The DC led Raven past Immigration as far as the main concourse.

'I think you upset him,' he said, and was gone.

The same girl was on duty at the BA reservations desk. Raven put the ticket in front of her.

'I won't be needing this after all.'

Her expression showed that she knew. 'I can't cash it in. It was paid for by credit card.'

'Just do whatever you have to,' he said, smiling. 'The name is John Raven.'

His next stop was the carpark across the bridge. The BMW had gone. He used a nearby phone and called his number. Page answered.

'What's happening?' Raven asked.

'Everything's cool,' Page replied.

'I'm on my way. Stay off the phone and don't leave the boat.'

He hailed a cab from the line waiting outside the terminal. It dropped him off on Chelsea Embankment. The BMW was back in its place in the cul-de-sac. Raven ran down the steps. The sitting-room door was open. Page was lying on one of the couches. The ashtray on the table in front of him was littered with cigarette butts. The car keys lay next to the ashtray.

Raven checked the answering machine. There were no fresh messages. He paused in the kitchen doorway.

'You want coffee or something?'

Page sat up straight. 'Coffee would be fine.'

Raven spooned Costa Rican instant into two cups, added milk and sugar and placed one in front of Page.

'I want you to tell me exactly what you saw from the balcony.'

Page had both hands round his cup. 'I saw you go past the security men. Then you went out of sight. All hell broke loose down below. Guys running round with walkie-talkies. The girl at the desk was talking to two of them.' He shrugged. 'I did what you told me to do – got out of there quickly. Nobody stopped me. Nobody even spoke to me.'

'You didn't see Manning?'

Page looked alarmed. 'You mean Manning was there?'

Raven explained what had happened beyond the screen. He made sure that he had held the other man's attention.

'Somebody called Manning last night, told him you were leaving the country this morning, gave the flight time and destination. Your name was on the ticket I bought. It wasn't me that Manning expected to collar. It was you. Only three people knew what was happening, Philip. Do you see what this means?'

The room was suddenly quiet. A police launch used its siren upstream.

Page's head sunk low on his chest.

'I can't believe this,' he said.

'You've got to face facts,' Raven urged. 'Somebody made a statement against you. Somebody had Marcus Poole killed and tried to set you up for it. Someone who wants to destroy you completely. Only three people knew that you were supposed to be on that plane. You, me and Henry Vyner.'

Page's face had lost colour under the sunburn. He shook his head slowly. 'I've known Henry Vyner all my life. We were at school together. He's Drusilla's godfather. The one person who's always stood by me.'

'Listen,' said Raven, 'I know what you're going through.' He lit a Gitane and passed it to Page. 'Betrayal's a hard one to handle. The thing is, I'm not involved emotionally, Philip. I see things clearly. Vyner isn't your friend, he's your enemy. He wants you destroyed. I think we both know why. He was in love with your wife.'

Page was still shaking his head, his eyes tightly shut.

Raven went on. 'He failed with Poole. But if you were caught trying to jump bail, you'd be a certainty for a very long sentence.'

Page removed his hands from his face. 'I feel gutted.'

'Now's the time to start fighting,' said Raven. 'For Drusilla as well as yourself. Look, we've come this far together. We've got to finish it. You're in court within hours. We've got to get that statement withdrawn before then.'

Page's smile was joyless. 'How do I do that – hold a gun to his head?'

'Call him now,' Raven said, dropping the phone in the other man's lap. 'Go ahead and dial. Tell him you have to see him right away. He'll be expecting to hear from you.'

Sweat glistened on Page's forehead. He took his time composing the number then spoke briefly. He replaced the handset.

'He can't come to London. He's sending the car for me.'

Raven opened a drawer in his desk and put a wristwatch and pocket calculator on the table. He slid back the top of the calculator, revealing two small batteries and a mini-cassette.

'The recording unit,' he explained. 'The cassette lasts half an hour on each side and the range is ten metres. There's no static. OK?'

Page nodded.

The wristwatch was a fake Cartier made in Taiwan. Raven

lifted the winding stem. 'That activates the speaker. All you're carrying is a watch and a pocket calculator. No problem.'

Page removed his own watch, substituting it with Raven's fake Cartier.

'I don't know,' he said doubtfully. 'Henry's no fool.'

'Forget it,' said Raven. 'He's your last and only friend. You're going to him out of desperation. Look, your whole life's been a gamble. Go for it.'

They talked for the next twenty minutes, Page doing most of the listening.

'I'd better go,' said Page. He looked at the watch and smiled.

Raven walked him as far as the steps. 'Come straight back here,' he warned. 'I'll be waiting. And good luck.'

An hour went by.

Chapter Eight

The housekeeper had cleaned the flat in Page's absence. His dirty linen had been whisked away, a suit brushed and returned to the wardrobe. He picked up a magazine but his mind kept wandering. What had happened that morning had left him deeply disturbed. Against every wish he found himself being convinced by Raven's logic. Who was there left he could trust?

He called the auction rooms. Drusilla was found and came to the phone, breathless and anxious.

'Where are you speaking from? What happened?'

'I'm at Embankment Gardens.'

'Thank God for that!' she exploded. 'I didn't know what to do last night. I was out of my mind. I found that message on my answering machine. You could at least have come to see me. Are you all right?'

'I just didn't want to have to explain, darling. Too difficult. I was going to make a run for it. I changed my mind at the last minute. I'm going down to the country to see Uncle Henry. He's sending the car for me.'

Her tone sharpened. 'But why didn't you tell me what was happening, Papa? Look, I have to talk to you.'

'OK. We'll meet on John Raven's boat. Why don't you go there when you've finished work? I should be back by then.'

He heard a voice call her name in the background.

'I have to go,' she said hurriedly. 'I'll see you later.'

He stood at the window, his memory stained with regret,

looking down at the cold fast-running river. Part of his brain hoped that the car would not come for him, that the showdown with Vyner was no more than a nightmare. The Bentley appeared minutes later. Page was on his way down before the door buzzer sounded.

Federico stood on the steps outside, a clean-shaven bandit in chauffeur's uniform. Page recalled that the man had once been a bodyguard in Marcos' Manila. Page wondered how much violence was left in the man's brain and body. Federico's loyalty to Vyner was unqualified. Page also wondered how much use Vyner had made of it.

They travelled without conversation, the driver handling the powerful car with a judicious blend of speed and caution. The road grew narrower once into Surrey, banks of snow encroaching on to the verges.

Scarclyff Manor stood in the ghost of pale sunshine, the scene of Drusilla's christening party. A sophisticated priest had officiated, drinking champagne afterwards at the reception. Page had been amused when he heard that Father Dunne had run off with his secretary three months later.

Maria opened the nail-studded doors, brown-skinned and smiling, attired in a blue uniform edged with white piping. She welcomed Page gladly.

'So long time!' she complained. 'How is your daughter?'

'She's fine,' he said shortly. He pulled the stem on the watch as he crossed the hallway. Maria opened the door on her left.

Vyner was standing in front of the log fire, the pug-dog snoring on a rug at his feet. His high-waisted grey flannel trousers were cut to conceal his belly. He wore a black knitted cardigan over a Turnbull and Asser country shirt.

His eyes held Page close. 'Do you want tea before the woman goes?'

Page made a sign of refusal. The door to the hallway was closed. The room was peaceful, the only noises those of the fire and the dog's noisy breathing.

'It didn't work out,' Page said, raising his head.

Vyner moved a hand, half-dismissal, half-benediction. A prince of the church with a bald head and an air of nobility.

'Maybe it's all for the best,' Vyner said softly.

'I hope so,' Page said uncertainly. He opened the lid of the silver box and extracted a cigarette. The watch on his right wrist peeped from his sleeve. It felt vibrant with electronic signals. It was difficult not to show his real feelings.

He nodded at the twelve-bore Purdey leaning against the panelled wall. 'I see you've still got your gun.'

Vyner toed the dog from the rug. It snuffled its way to its lair behind the curtain.

'Oddly enough it came back this morning. There was something wrong with the choke.'

The shotgun had been a present from Page on Vyner's fortieth birthday. It seemed a long time ago.

Vyner's jowls quivered with merriment. 'I'm still no better a shot, I'm afraid. But then as you always said, the chase is more important than the kill.'

'I said that?' queried Page. 'Another one of my bullshit one-liners.'

He was seeing Vyner down the years. A private man, tolerant, all things to his friends. A secret man, withdrawn from publicity or observation.

Page lunged into his preamble. The script was entirely Raven's.

'Raven was supposed to take care of the passport. He didn't turn up at the airport. I thought he was genuine. But you can never tell.'

Vyner bent down and stirred up the fire with a poker. His face was flushed when he straightened his back and turned.

'I was expecting a call from Havana. Too bad.'

'Too bad,' agreed Page. 'I suppose I'm lucky to get out of it without the police knowing. I got as far as the BA reservations desk. I had my ticket and the boarding card. All I needed was Raven to show with the passport.'

'Did Drusilla know?' Vyner asked, mopping his neck with a blue cotton handkerchief.

'No,' said Page. 'I was going to wait until I got to Havana.'

'An odd place to choose,' Vyner said.

'An unlikely place. That's what Raven said. Once you're there you're invisible. The Cubans don't belong to Interpol. That's what he said.'

'So what happens now?' Vyner asked. His eyes rested everywhere except on Page's face.

Page's shoulders rose and fell. 'I just have to take my chances. And I wouldn't assess them too highly.'

Vyner clucked his tongue a few times. 'You've got the best lawyer in London. If Horobin can't get you off the hook then nobody can.'

'It's Horobin who doesn't fancy my chances,' said Page. 'You heard the latest about this statement they're putting in. The witness doesn't have to appear in court. They'll claim he's in fear of his life.'

They looked at one another briefly. Vyner tilted his head, firelight shining on his forehead and nose. 'Drusilla said you were asking about those papers again. The ones you left with Marian.'

'That's right,' said Page. 'I'm sure there's stuff there that could be used in rebuttal.'

'I've already told you,' said Vyner. 'I never saw any papers. Marian certainly didn't mention any documents, papers, whatever they were. I supervised the move from Chesham Street to Dolphin Square. If there'd been anything there I'd have seen it. I saw nothing.'

A year ago, a month ago, even a day ago, Page would have believed him. Now he knew that Vyner was lying. It was the moment to start goading him.

'No one could have done more for me than you have,' said Page. His voice was beginning to sound false to his own ears. 'You've been one in a million. It's strange, thinking back. You're the one Marian should have married.'

Vyner's face wore an unaccustomed flush. 'How do you mean?'

'She was in love with you, Henry.'

'Me? Don't be ridiculous. For me she was always your wife.'

'Having been your girlfriend to start with. You were well out of it, Henry.'

Vyner stared hard at him, his massive chin lifted challengingly.

'That's the way life is,' Page continued. 'The woman was a slut. You weren't the only one she fancied. Have you any idea how it feels to lie in bed and know that your wife wants to screw your friends, Henry? I'm sorry to disillusion you. She was a drunk and a whore. I'd have left her years ago if it hadn't been for Drusilla.'

Vyner's jowls twitched as though struck with some raging toothache. His eyes seemed reduced in size to prunes of intense dislike. 'But you never said anything. Not to her or to me.'

Page juggled his hands. 'I resented you, Henry. You fucked up my marriage but we all had to get on with our lives. I'll tell you the truth. I was glad when I heard that Marian had killed herself. It was the best thing that could have happened for everyone.'

Vyner's stomach swelled as he breathed in deeply. 'You're maligning a good woman. OK, you want it, I'll give it to you.'

He towered in anger, his whole body shaking. 'I was your friend but you had ceased to be mine. I hated the way you used charm when others got punished. You had no feeling for anyone but yourself. Marian *did* give me those papers to destroy. She died thinking I'd done it. But I had them. And when I looked through the diary, I suddenly realised what those dates meant. I was just biding my time until the right moment came to use them. You're looking at the architect of your downfall. Marian was the only person I've ever loved.

You ruined her. And that's what I'm going to do to you. That's why Marcus Poole died. I'm the one who had him killed. Raven managed to get you out of that one. But now it's over. I'm going to see you in jail for a long, long, time.'

Page rang the bell near the door. Maria knocked, then her head appeared.

'Get me a car from the station please, Maria. I want it to take me back to London. And I want it immediately.'

He walked into the hallway cloakroom and ran cold water on his face. He looked like a man who has seen his own ghost.

When he returned to the drawing room, Vyner was sitting down with the pug in his lap. He spoke as a man near the end of his tether.

'I'm glad you came here, Philip. Revenge is never as sweet as when the victim knows where it's coming from.'

Page looked at the gun leaning against the wall. 'Have you given even the smallest last thought to Drusilla?'

Vyner chuckled. 'I'll be sitting in court, holding her hand. Your loyal friend to the last. Only the police know who made the statement. Don't waste your time trying to poison her mind. She won't believe you.'

Tyres crunched on the gravel outside. Page turned away from the window.

'You know what they say in California, Henry? The show isn't over until the fat lady sings. Remember that when you're trying to sleep tonight.'

Maria was waiting outside in the hallway. The front door was open. He slipped a ten-pound note into her hand.

'Goodbye, Maria.'

He walked out to the waiting taxi without glancing back at the windows. The last battle was always the one that counted.

He climbed into old-fashioned creaking leather. 'Chelsea,' he ordered. 'I'll tell you where once we're in London.'

The driver was mercifully taciturn. As soon as they were

into the woods Page drew the calculator from his pocket. The mini-cassette was still turning. He played back a few turns until Vyner's voice sounded. Then he dropped the set back into his pocket, closed his eyes and did his best to make his mind blank.

It was a quarter past five by the time they reached Chelsea Embankment. He paid the driver, used his keys and stood in the silent hallway until he heard the car being driven away. Then he let himself out on the street again and walked west towards the houseboats. He was suddenly apprehensive. Vyner was dangerous, still capable of anything. For that matter, so was the chauffeur.

Tidal water was surging up river, slapping against the jetty. The overhead sodium lights came on with startling clarity. Roosting gulls paid no attention.

The sitting room door was open, Raven waiting inside.

'Drusilla's here,' Raven said quickly. 'Come on in.'

Page's daughter was sitting in Raven's favourite chair, still wearing her work clothes. Her red hair was held back on her neck with an ivory skewer. Her coat was draped on the back of a couch. He bent down and kissed her with a feeling of guilt.

Her voice was just audible. 'Hello, Papa.' Her eyes were clouded with misery.

'I've told her,' said Raven. He shut the door to the deck. The mooring-chains groaned as they strained against the current.

Page unstrapped the watch and put it on the table next to the calculator.

Raven extracted the tape. His Bang & Olufsen accepted the mini-cassette. He started the machine and adjusted the tone and volume.

Vyner's voice sounded in the two high-fidelity speakers. Drusilla was nibbling a cuticle. Raven sat down, his face expressionless. Page remembered the shotgun leaning against the drawing-room wall. He thought of blowing Vyner's skull asunder. He bent forward, hearing Vyner's tone change as he gloated over his betrayal.

When the tape stopped, Drusilla swung round on Page, hands clenched tightly. 'How could you *say* those awful things about my mother?'

It was Raven who answered. 'He was only saying what I told him to say. The whole thing was staged. It was the only way we could get Vyner to crack.'

'All those lies,' she said, unappeased.

'For God's sake, grow up,' Raven snapped. 'You think it was easy for your father? Look at his face!'

Drusilla's hand touched Page's arm very gently. 'I'm sorry,' she whispered.

Raven was standing by the music centre. He rapped on the shelf for attention.

'OK. Now, listen, both of you. We're going to play the tape back to Vyner. I mean you are!' He pointed to Page. 'You know what to say. Don't get involved in discussions. Either he withdraws the statement or you use the tape. No compromise, no concession. Go ahead.'

Page dialled Scarclyff Manor. 'It's me again,' he said when Vyner answered. 'There's something I want you to hear.' He carried the phone to the speaker.

The tape started to roll. Raven was leaning back on the cushions. Drusilla beside him still nibbling the end of her finger.

The only sound in the earpiece was Vyner's amplified breathing. He seemed to be having trouble with it. Then the line was disconnected.

'He hung up on me,' Page said, looking across at Raven.

'Don't sell him short,' Raven said, taking the cassette from the music centre. 'He's going to start covering his tracks. I'll have this tape copied. There's a place on the King's Road that stays open until nine. Horobin gets one copy. One goes to the Director of Public Prosecutions. The original we keep as insurance.'

Drusilla was huddled over, hiding her tears. She moved quickly towards the phone. Raven grabbed her wrist.

'What the hell do you think you're doing?'

She broke free from his grip, her expression determined. She held the phone tight to her chest. 'I want him to hear my voice,' she insisted. 'I want him to know how I feel. Please don't stop me,' she pleaded.

The two men looked at one another.

'Go ahead,' said Raven.

Her chin tilted aggressively as the dialling tone sounded. 'Maria? It's Drusilla. Let me talk to Uncle Henry, please.'

She replaced the phone and shrugged. 'She said he's not there. I don't believe her.'

'Did she know it was you?' Raven asked.

'I told her,' said Drusilla. 'She might not have understood.' Her eyes glittered with unshed tears. Her make-up was already streaked.

Page put his arm around her shoulders and drew her close.

She stirred in his embrace. 'Why don't we just tell the police and *basta*? Tell them what happened?'

'Because we don't trust the police,' said Raven.

Drusilla's eyes were bright. 'Uncle Henry's been lying and cheating for years.' It sounded like a public announcement to Page's ears. 'Turning me against my father. The awful thing is that Mamma believed every word of it. She didn't even have the consolation of knowing the truth. I hate him! He's evil. He *deserves* to be punished. I wish he was dead.'

Raven slipped into his lumberjacket. Beyond the open door lights twinkled on the opposite bank of the river.

'There is just one possible problem,' he said, holding the cassette in the air. 'The police don't give up easily. There may be some legal quibble involved. I mean how we obtained the statement in the first place.'

'You think so?' Page's expression was suddenly downcast.

'May be,' emphasised Raven. 'But I doubt it. They're using

wire-taps all the time without asking too many questions. See if you can get hold of Horobin while I'm out. Ask if we can go round and see him. I shouldn't be long.'

The door slammed at the foot of the steps. Page withdrew his arm from his daughter and lifted the phone. There was no reply from Horobin's chambers. His home number produced a recorded message. Page put the phone down.

'No answer,' he said. They seemed to be talking in clichés. Drusilla snuggled closer again.

'I know just how hard this is for you,' Page said, stroking her hair. 'I'm still finding it difficult to believe. I don't understand how he was able to hide his hatred for so many years. What the hell did I do to him?'

She raised her head. 'That's easy. He was jealous. You were everything he always wanted to be and wasn't. Worst of all you took Mamma away from him. You know what I think was the final straw? You saying Mamma was in love with him. It was a glimpse of what might have been.'

They sat quiet in a newly forged closeness. Talk for the moment was useless. Raven's footsteps sounded outside on the deck. Page unlocked the door.

Raven came in, shivering theatrically. He was carrying a plastic bag. TOWER OF BABEL. ALL FORMS OF ELECTRONIC EQUIPMENT.

The buzzer sounded again. Raven hurried to the far end of the room and opened the curtain slightly. He swung round, his expression alarmed.

'It's Manning,' he said hurriedly. 'He must have been on my tail. Not one word about Vyner.'

He released the catch on the gangway door and locked the plastic bag in the desk. He stood in the open doorway, his shadow slanting across the deck.

Manning came in, red-nosed and blowing. He was holding the hat with the burn in the brim.

'I thought I might find you here,' he said, looking directly at Page. He turned to Drusilla and Raven. 'I'm sorry for the intrusion. I wanted this visit to be discreet. That's why I left my sergeant outside in the car.' He switched his regard back to Page. 'I've got bad news for you. Your bail's no good any more.'

Page's mouth opened but no words came out. His vocal chords were refusing to work.

Raven took charge. 'How do you mean no good any more?' he demanded indignantly.

Manning composed his regard, dropping his voice dramatically. 'Henry Vyner's dead. We got the news half an hour ago. Killed himself with a shotgun. The servants called the local police. They got in touch with us. And that's why I'm here. Mr Vyner's surety is no longer valid. Dead men have no credibility.'

Raven backed off towards his desk, trying to remember whether or not he had locked it.

'Do Mr Page's lawyers know about this?'

Detective Superintendent Manning's attitude had changed since that morning. He was not only the bearer of bad news but a man who above all did his duty. He pinched his mouth disapprovingly.

'Both gentlemen have been informed. They're on their way to Chelsea police station.'

'Surely somebody else could provide bail?' It was Drusilla, still sitting close to her father.

'That may well be, miss,' said Manning. 'But it won't be tonight, that's for sure. In any case your father's due in court in the morning. Things should have been straightened out by then.'

The top of Raven's desk was unlocked. He delved inside. When he turned, he was holding one of the cassettes.

'I've got no quarrel with you, superintendent. You're only doing your job. But I wouldn't want to see you make a fool of yourself. Listen to this as soon as you get to the police station. It's important.'

Manning weighed the tape in his hand, his eyes large with sudden suspicion. 'What is it?'

'It's a record of a conversation that took place between Henry Vyner and Philip Page. It was recorded this afternoon at Scarclyff Manor. Another copy's going to the Director of Public Prosecutions by courier. And remember what you said earlier. Dead men have no credibility.'

Manning was clearly perturbed. He seemed on the brink of refusing the tape, then dropped it in his overcoat pocket.

'OK,' he said to Page. 'If you're ready, let's go.'

Page hauled himself up and put his arm round his daughter. 'Don't worry, darling. You stay with John and do what he says. I'll see you in court in the morning.'

Manning clapped on his trilby. He touched the brim, looking across at Drusilla. 'Good night, miss.' He said nothing to Raven.

Their footsteps receded along the deck. Then the door banged at the end of the gangway.

Drusilla unpinned her hair and shook it free. Her small smile came and went. 'It's weird. I feel almost relieved. As though the uncertainty's over.'

She looked at him for confirmation.

He was back at his desk, another cassette in his hand.

'It's too late to bluff,' he said. 'We've got to get this tape to the DPP's office.'

He telephoned Kirstie's radio-cab service, gave them her account number and address. 'The taxi's on its way,' he said, putting the phone down.

He scribbled a note on the boat-headed stationery.

Evidence in the trial of Regina v Philip Page.
Horseferry Road Magistrates' Court.

He put the note and cassette in a brown padded envelope. 'I'll be back in a minute,' he promised.

He climbed the steps to the Embankment and checked the pub carpark opposite. The only vehicle there belonged to the landlord. A cab turned right on Oakley Street and came in the direction of the boats, indicator blinking. The driver lowered a window.

'Name of Raven?'

Raven gave him the envelope. 'Twenty-six Queen Anne's Gate. The office is sure to be closed but there'll be someone there, someone in security.'

The driver grinned, offering a voucher for Raven to sign. 'Sure it isn't a bomb of some kind?'

Raven scribbled his signature. 'Not the sort you have in mind, anyway.'

Raven closed the sitting-room door behind him and put on J. J. Cale singing 'Okie'. He lowered the volume.

'What do you want to do, Drusilla, go out and eat or what?'

She kicked off her pumps and drew her legs up under her. 'I don't want to go home yet, that's for sure. What I'd really like to do is stay here and talk.'

'Then that's what we'll do,' Raven said cheerfully. 'Just let me make a couple more calls.'

There was no reply from Loeb's number. Raven called Paris. Maureen O'Callaghan answered.

'No, he's not here. I've no idea . . . He's supposed to be coming back for supper.'

'Give him this message,' said Raven. 'It was Vyner who made the statement. He killed himself this afternoon.'

The line was suddenly distant and hollow. Then Maureen was back. 'You did say "killed himself"?'

'Yes,' said Raven. 'Tell Patrick he can come back whenever he likes.'

He put the phone down firmly. She was a skilled cross-examiner.

'OK,' he said, looking across at Drusilla. 'I think we've pulled it off. This calls for a celebration.'

There was a second bottle of Blanquette de Limoux in the refrigerator. He got rid of the cork and carried the wine and two glasses into the sitting room.

Drusilla had used the time to repair her make-up. She lifted her glass.

'Happy days!'

'Happy days,' he repeated.

Her eyes strayed to Kirstie's picture on top of the desk. Drusilla looked at him over her glass.

'May I ask you a personal question?'

'Go ahead,' he said, perching on the arm of the couch. 'If I don't know the answer, I'll invent one.'

'Are you still in love with your wife?'

The question was totally unexpected. It was as though shared peril had forged a new intimacy between them.

'Do I love Kirstie?' he repeated. He affected to think. 'Well, she's stubborn and argumentative. She likes peanut butter and has never as much as sewn one button on a shirt for me. But then she does make me laugh and most of the time she's understanding. Yes, I love her.'

She wriggled sideways on the couch to get a better look at his face.

'I wonder if love's the same for everyone.'

J. J. Cale's smoky voice sang of Cajun women. Raven emptied his glass, the bubbles exploding high in his nose.

'I don't think I've ever thought about it,' he said. 'I can only speak for myself. I seem to have been in love many times, but Kirstie's the only one I remember. What makes you ask? Have you got somebody special in mind?'

She looked across at the desk again as though comparing herself with the photograph.

'Me?' she replied, turning towards him again. 'I'm not really sure. My problem is I'm a romantic.'

He topped up their glasses. The bubbles made him want to sneeze. He was about to say something stupid, offer a peep inside his box of secrets.

'There's only one way to preserve romance. People need lots of space. There's nothing that kills romance as quickly as too much togetherness. All those confidences shared in a moment of passion have a way of coming back like boomerangs.'

'That's sad,' she said, moving her head from side to side. She sat up a little straighter and nibbled again at a cuticle, still looking at him.

'I'm sorry,' he shrugged. 'But you did ask me a question.'

She put her empty glass down very carefully. 'Ah well, I can always dream, I suppose. You're a good man, John Raven. There ought to be someone like you in every girl's life.'

'You mean a sort of honorary godfather?' He had no right to keep this conversation going, but there was no chance of stopping himself.

She moved her head and hands in dissent. 'Not quite. I'm talking about someone you can really trust. A woman I know says that's the best form of love. Friendship. There's no sex involved.'

He had a sudden glimpse of his wife in the house in York Mills. Red-brick homes nestling in frozen snowbanks. Tree-lined avenues freshly gritted. Calm, undisturbed voices engaged in matters of parochial concern. He changed the subject deliberately.

'Do you know what you should do when all this is over? Take a long trip with your father. Somewhere like the South Pacific. You're all he's got left and vice-versa.'

Her feet touched the floor. Her smile was provocative. 'I think I'm getting a little bit drunk. I can't take very much.'

'Get to know one another better,' he added.

She thought about that for a moment. 'Henry Vyner said they'd make Papa bankrupt. Or was that just another of his lies?'

'They might well be able to do it,' said Raven.

She was sitting on the edge of the couch, her skirt hiked up, revealing her thighs.

'Did he really take all that money?' she asked.

There was a glimpse of bare flesh. The black silk expanse was stockings not tights. He averted his eyes.

138

'That's what he says,' Raven answered. 'My guess is that a lot of it's gone. For one thing, he bought that place in California. And don't forget it was your father who funded the trust. Vyner was only the figurehead.'

He consulted the clock. 'Shall we go out and get something to eat?'

The slight flush on her face made her freckles stand out. Her tone was indifferent. 'I don't really care. If you have eggs I could scramble them.'

'Eggs we've always got,' he said briskly. 'Come with me and I'll show you.'

She padded after him into the kitchen, shoeless. Her attention was immediately caught by the pottery displayed on the fumed-oak Welsh dresser. She picked up a figure of a jaguar with an eagle's head.

'Is this Central American?'

He put a carton of free-range eggs on the table. 'You've got a good eye.'

She replaced the figure carefully. 'I enjoy my job and I'm still learning. Was I right?'

He cracked six eggs into the bowl and put butter and milk on the table. 'I like my eggs runny.'

'Was I right?' she repeated.

'Honduran,' he said. 'A friend of ours, Maggie Sanchez, gave them to us. She's half-Spanish, half-Guatemalan.'

She stood at the kitchen table, her eyes ranging the shelves and cupboards. 'Have you got a mixer?'

'I use a fork,' he replied. He took one from the table drawer.

'I know that name,' she said, reflectively. 'Maggie Sanchez. Isn't she a model? I've seen her picture in *Vogue*.'

'Kirstie took the pictures,' said Raven. 'Maggie's boyfriend was a chum of mine. He died a sudden and violent death.'

She had donned Mrs Burrows' checked overall. 'You mix with some colourful people.'

He excused himself and went back to the sitting room.

There was a box of Swedish candles in one of the cupboards, golden wax that burned with a clear aromatic flame. He set the table. Stubby silver candlesticks, a Victorian cloth and napkins.

He took a clean pair of pyjamas from a drawer in his bedroom, a *Variq* overnight kit from Kirstie's store in the bathroom cabinet. Toothbrush and paste, comb and face tissues. He left the articles on one of the beds in the guest room. He drew the curtains. The bedside lamp shone on the flower-sprigged pillow and duvet cover. His smile was unconscious.

The smell of coffee led him back to the sitting room. Coffee was percolating on the side table. Drusilla came in. She put a plate of buttered-toast fingers on the table, removed the top of the dish with a flourish.

'*Voila*! I hope it is to monsieur's liking.'

He tasted a mouthful of scrambled egg and made a circle with thumb and forefinger.

'Perfect,' he judged. 'How much would you charge to stay on?'

'I don't think your wife would approve of that.' It was hard to tell if she was teasing or serious.

He spoke through a mouthful of food. 'Kirstie knows me too well. I'm a model husband.'

'I doubt that,' she said. 'Seriously. No woman should be that sure of a man.'

He moved one of the candlesticks the better to see her. 'I've made up a bed for you in the guest room. That's if you feel like staying. It's entirely up to you.'

Her green eyes were gold-flecked in the candlelight.

'I'd like that,' she said. 'I'd sooner not stay alone in the flat tonight.'

The phone rang before he could comment. He wiped his mouth hurriedly and took the call in the bedroom. It could be Kirstie. It was Loeb. He was with Horobin. They had just left Chelsea police station. Manning had played the tape to them. Horobin was on his way to the Home Office.

Raven went back to the sitting room. 'That was Loeb. They've heard the tape. Horobin's got another meeting at the Home Office early tomorrow morning. They're trying to work out some sort of compromise.'

Doubt clouded her face. 'What does that mean?'

'A compromise with the prosecution and Consol Electric. They're the ones who've lost the money. Horobin thinks they might settle for what they can claw back.'

'Can they do that?'

He drank the coffee she had poured. 'They can do anything they like, Drusilla. All we can do is hope for the best.'

Her fingers found his across the table and locked tight. 'OK, I've decided. I'll stay on here and work as long as you'll be my godfather.'

They finished their meal in a leisurely manner. Drusilla cleared the table. He heard her washing up in the kitchen. She came back trailing her scent with her.

'It's eleven o'clock,' Raven said, turning his wrist. 'Bed-time. Get yourself a glass of juice and I'll show you your room.'

She went back to the kitchen and opened the fridge.

'Mrs Burrows squeezes fresh orange juice every day,' he encouraged.

Drusilla filled a glass. He blew out the candles and shot the bolts on the sitting room door. She picked up her pumps and followed him down the corridor. He nodded across at the bed.

'There should be everything there that you need. The bathroom's next door. You can go first.' He smiled. 'I've still got one more call to make.'

She held the pyjama jacket up in front of her. It was several sizes too big.

'Good night, Drusilla,' he said.

She stood on her toes, took his face in her hands and

kissed him full on the lips. 'Good night, godfather. Sweet dreams.'

Back in his own room, he set the alarm for seven o'clock in the morning. It was no time to rely on his own built-in system.

Water was running in the bathtub next door. He sprawled on the bed. It was six o'clock in Toronto. He lay on his back, the phone on his chest.

His wife's voice came clearly, borne on an electronic rush of whispers. 'My God, it's you again!'

A picture of them both on the deck of a boat in the Aegean stood on the dressing table.

'I've got a confession to make,' he announced. 'There's a girl sleeping in the guest room.'

'That bimbo,' she said tartly. 'The Page girl. Why is she sleeping there? Hasn't she got a bed of her own?'

'Because she's a worried lady,' he said. 'Her father's in court in the morning. It's no time to spend the night alone. I just thought I'd let you know before Mrs Burrows does.'

His wife made a sound of disdain. 'I'd be the last person she'd tell. She'd be delighted to find you in bed with someone else.'

'But she won't,' Raven said. 'I'll call you same time tomorrow. Good night and God bless!'

He waited until he heard the bathroom door being opened and closed. He went in to brush his teeth. The towel that Drusilla had used was on the side of the tub, neatly folded. The light in the guest room was already extinguished.

He lay in the darkness, his brain accepting the sound-pattern of familiar knocks and clatter, the dull roar of the traffic up on the Embankment. Part of his brain told him that he need not have slept alone. How much of that was wishful thinking he would never know. But it was good to believe that he had resisted temptation.

Chapter Nine

Raven heard Drusilla moving about shortly after his alarm had gone off. He pulled on his robe and went into the bathroom. The door to the guest room was open. Pillowcases, the sheet and duvet cover were folded neatly at the foot of the bed. Apart from the smell of the scent she used there was no indication that she had spent the night there.

He shut the door quietly. The sitting room was in darkness. It was a moment before he made out Drusilla at the far end of the room, in front of a gap in the curtains. She was fully dressed, just standing there staring out at the start of another grey day.

She jumped as she heard his voice.

'Hi there! How did you sleep?'

She spoke as though she preferred not to remember. 'OK, I suppose. Would you like me to make some breakfast?'

'I'll do it,' he replied. 'You want coffee or tea?'

'Tea, please. Nothing to eat. I'm not hungry.'

She was strangely subdued as she followed him into the kitchen. He filled the kettle. They both sat down at the table.

'What's the matter, Drusilla?' he asked.

She raised her head very slowly as if afraid of meeting his gaze. 'I'm sorry about last night. I drank too much. I don't like making a fool of myself.'

'You didn't,' he assured her. 'And for God's sake stop worrying. The worst is over.'

Her eyes were miserable. 'I never felt so much alone in my life,' she said sadly.

The water boiled. He made Earl Grey in two cups and set one in front of her.

'You're not alone! That's nonsense. You've just got your father back again.'

'That's what's worrying me,' she replied. 'I just can't believe that they'll let him go. Look, I can understand how Papa got into this in the first place. It was the way he lived, the way he looked at things. The fact remains that he did take the money.'

He lit the first cigarette of the day. 'Your father's got the best lawyers possible. Things are out of our hands now, Drusilla. We've just got to hope for the best. But there's one thing I want you to know. I'm on your side too.'

Her smile came and went quickly. 'I know that. You're the only real friend we have left.'

He finished his tea and put the cup in the sink. 'Loeb said not to bother getting to the court before half past eleven. That means we've got over three hours to kill.'

She took a quick look in her hand-mirror and reached for her coat. 'I think I'll go home and change. What time do you want me back here?'

He walked to the deck with her. 'Eleven o'clock. That gives us plenty of leeway.'

Lights shone on his neighbour's boat. The Great Dane was sniffing the breeze and barking.

'Are you going to be all right?' Raven queried.

'Why not?' she said indifferently. 'It's only a ten-minute walk.' She lifted a hand and was gone.

He collected the post and the newspapers from the box at the foot of the steps. The sound of a child practising scales on a piano drifted across the water. Gulls rose in flocks, shrieking discordantly. He closed the sitting-room door and glanced through the post. There were a couple of bills, an invitation to the Black Bull Gallery, a buff envelope for Kirstie from the

Inland Revenue. There was no mention of Page's appearance in court in the newspapers.

He shaved and put on a double-breasted blue suit that was sixteen years old. He chose a white shirt and a silk tie to go with it, a pair of hand-made loafers. He ought to invest in some new clothes. Everything he owned dated back to the Seventies. The trousers were a little tight round the waist. The roll of flesh there was what Kirstie called his 'love-handles'. He had a sudden thought that neither Kirstie nor he would ever know what might have happened the previous night. He had woken with the need to feel virtuous.

He hurried into the bedroom. The phone was ringing. It was Patrick O'Callaghan, his voice sharp with indignation. It was all very well for Raven to act as though nothing had happened. He didn't seem to realise the agony O'Callaghan had had to endure. People like Page should be under control. And so on.

Raven listened until he ran out of patience. 'Let me remind you of something,' he said, interrupting. 'You're the one who started all this! You came here in fear of your life, desperate. You pleaded with me and I was sorry for you. Remember that before you start shouting.'

'I am not shouting,' the lawyer yelled. 'You're enjoying every minute of this. It's always the same. You don't need to go to the theatre. You live it!'

Raven sucked in a deep breath. 'You're a very selfish person at times, Patrick. My advice to you is stay put in Paris. Have a relaxed weekend. Tell Maureen the truth, for God's sake. She'll understand. And don't worry about your work. You're not indispensable. You were never indispensable. Nobody is.'

Raven sat up straight. This myth about his enjoyment of drama was an invention of Kirstie's. Whatever the truth, he was not likely to change.

The phone rang again at ten past eleven. 'I've got a taxi waiting downstairs,' said Drusilla. 'I'm on my way now.'

'I'll be at the top of the steps,' Raven promised.

The taxi drew up as he reached the Embankment. Raven climbed in beside Drusilla. As far as he could determine she was still wearing the same clothes. She must have had another reason for going home. Her hand stole into his and gripped tightly.

Business at Horseferry Road Magistrates' Court had already terminated. A few confirmed misery-watchers and some passers-by milled about on the pavement outside, inflamed by the presence of reporters and photographers, a television crew.

Raven pushed money at the taxi driver and made a run through the crowd, dragging Drusilla after him. Once inside the building, they hurried into the lift. He pressed the third-floor button.

'OK?' he said, looking at her anxiously.

She put on a pair of dark glasses and nodded. 'Just don't leave me,' she pleaded.

The lift stopped. They walked out on to the concourse. He had been here so many times in the past. Three of the courts were closed. The door to the fourth stood open. Loeb and Horobin were standing near by, deep in conversation. Loeb broke away as he saw Drusilla and Raven.

'Could I have a word?' he said to Drusilla. 'Alone,' he added significantly.

Raven sat on a bench while they conversed, Drusilla constantly looking back over her shoulder at Raven. The two lawyers walked into the open courtroom. Drusilla returned to Raven.

He heaved himself up. 'What was all that about?'

'There's no time to explain,' she said quickly. 'I'll tell you later. That's where we're supposed to go.' She pointed at the door in front of them.

'OK,' Raven said. 'Let's show solidarity.'

Chapter Ten

Page had been in the cells at Horseferry Road for the last two and a half hours. Horobin and Loeb had visited him the previous night at the police station, Horobin coming straight from a meeting at the Home Office, attended by Miss Lassiter, the woman who was prosecuting Page's case. Horobin had delivered a short lecture on the sanctity of private property and the disastrous effect of major fraud in the City. The value of Consol Electric shares had decreased during the last three years. The news of Vyner's suicide and the impending withdrawal of his statement meant the possibility of some sort of compromise. The QC had departed, leaving three packs of Sullivan Powell *Sub Rosa* and a glimmer of hope for his client.

Now it was almost twenty past eleven. Page had not moved on the bench where he sat, as close to the door as was possible. The door opened suddenly. A cop with a grey crewcut crooked a finger at Page.

'You're on, mate!'

They walked side by side, the jailer swinging his keys on a chain. The lift was littered with the debris of a hundred trips made that morning. Cigarette butts, chewing-gum wrappers, bus tickets. They emerged on the third floor. A cleaner was mopping the floor of the concourse. Page's escort led the way through the empty courtroom and knocked on a door behind the magistrates' bench. He moved to one side allowing Page to go in. The door closed quietly again.

It was a large room with pictures of bygone magistrates hanging on the walls, wearing stiff collars and side whiskers. There were shelves full of legal tomes, cumbersome filing cabinets, a desk with a couple of telephones. Space had been made for a table to be placed lengthways across the room. Five people were sitting round the table.

There were three empty chairs.

The man standing at the far end introduced himself. 'I'm Robert Bruce, chief clerk to the magistrates.' He spoke with an Edinburgh accent, a neat brown-haired man in clothing that matched. His face looked ungiven to laughter. 'Please take a seat, Mr Page.'

Page sat down. Raven was on his left. Beyond that was Drusilla. She blew a quick kiss at her father. Horobin inclined his head, the customary rosebud in his lapel. Miss Lassiter was wearing a knitted wool suit and Christian Dior-framed spectacles. Detective Superintendent Manning sat on Miss Lassiter's left.

The chief clerk called for attention. 'I think we all know why we're here.' His voice held a faint note of disapproval.

'Hold it a minute,' said Page. He pointed at the man on his right. 'I don't know this gentleman.'

'Garth Munster,' said the stranger. He was dressed in varying shades of blue: suit, shirt and tie. He looked to be in his early forties and his smile meant nothing. 'I represent Consol Electric.'

'Yes,' said the chief clerk. 'Exactly. The purpose of this meeting is to discuss certain proposals that have been made. I should point out that this is in no sense prejudicial to Mr Page's position. A proposal has been made. It is up to Mr Page to accept or decline it. This meeting is taking place under conditions laid down by the Home Office. Miss Lassiter?'

The bobbing up and down was over. People spoke from their chairs. The barrister spoke with her eyes on the ceiling.

'My instructions are clear and precise. I intend asking for leave to withdraw the proceedings against Mr Page.'

Page looked the length of the table. Raven's wink was the quickest move of an eyelid.

Horobin nodded.

'Which leaves you, Mr Munster,' said the chief clerk.

The corporation lawyer looked through his briefcase until he found what he wanted. He placed a document on the table in front of him and donned reading spectacles.

'As you know, I represent Consol Electric. The disposition of the case against Mr Page does not fall within my province. However, not so the money concerned. We offer no objection to whatever course the authorities may decide to take, subject to the following conditions.'

He tapped the papers in front of him.

'Mr Page will provide a full statement of affairs: a disclosure of all assets obtained by him after Consol Electric's purchase of his company, Pantile HiTek Limited. In addition to this, we will require a declaration of Mr Page's intent to repay such moneys as may not be forthcoming during the initial stages. Consol Electric also reserves the right to bring suit against Mr Page in the civil courts in order to recover any possible shortfall. Considering all the circumstances, we consider this to be a generous offer.'

He passed the document along the table. Page took a look at it. 'I don't understand a word of this jargon.'

'I've read it,' Horobin put in quickly. 'My advice is to sign.'

The room was suddenly quiet. All heads turned in Page's direction. He breathed in hard through his nose. He was forty-seven years old and a survivor.

'Why not?' he said finally. 'I can always start over again.'

He signed with Munster's gold Shaeffer. Raven added his signature as witness. Munster put the document back in his briefcase, rose and looked round the table.

'I'll send you copies,' he said to Horobin. 'I bid you good day.'

He disappeared through the door to the courtroom. The chief clerk called the meeting to order.

'Very well, all that seems to be in order. If you people want to go through to the courtroom, I'll let the magistrate know that we're ready.'

Drusilla was close as Page walked through. The grey-haired jailer stood near the dock as Page stepped forward. Horobin and Loeb took their places in front of the magistrates' bench, Miss Lassiter and Detective Superintendent Manning on the other side of the aisle.

The magistrate bustled in and sat down, dwarfed in the ponderous chair. He was a man in his sixties with neat silver hair and bristling eyebrows.

'All right,' he said briskly. 'Let's get on with it.' The chief clerk and the court reporter sat below him. The press bench and public gallery were empty.

Miss Lassiter seemed as anxious to hurry things along as the magistrate. 'Your Honour, my instructions are to offer no further evidence in this case.'

The magistrate made a bold stroke of his pen. 'Mr Horobin?'

Horobin came to his feet, fingers straying to the rose in his lapel. 'With Your Honour's permission, I ask for a dismissal.'

The magistrate leaned down and had a few words with the chief clerk. He straightened his back and spoke with distaste.

'I disapprove strongly of this court's time being wasted like this. The prisoner is discharged and I make no order as to costs.'

There was general shuffling of feet as the magistrate left the courtroom. Manning came forward, offering Page's passport.

'No hard feelings, I hope?'

Page ignored the outstretched hand, took a quick look at his passport and put it away in his pocket.

'No hard feelings,' he said. 'I just hope I never see you again.'

Manning shrugged. 'The press are still waiting outside.

The officer will let you out the back way.' He indicated the crop-haired jailer.

Horobin and Loeb took their leave, actors acknowledging applause that was merited. Raven, Page and Drusilla walked out to the concourse. The police officer stood some yards away. Drusilla pulled her father down on a bench. Raven sat down with them.

'I've got a surprise for you,' Drusilla said to her father. Page searched her green eyes for a sign, but there was none. The cleaner was still mopping the floor at the far end of the concourse. Drusilla's eyes never left her father's face.

'Did you know that Uncle Henry made a will in my favour? It was just after Mamma died.'

Page shook his head. 'He never told me.'

'He tried to change the will after you played the tape back to him. Maria and her husband were witnesses. He left everything to the Battersea Dogs' Home. That was just half an hour before he killed himself.'

He took her hand quickly. 'We never needed his money,' he said consolingly. 'And we don't need it now. We'll get by. Don't worry.'

Raven broke in, smiling. 'That's not the point. A will needs two witnesses to be valid. Both witnesses have to sign in each other's presence. And the testator's of course. Maria had already signed. Then came this phone call. Maria left the room to answer it. When she came back her husband had signed in her absence.'

'So?'

A hint of glee capered in Raven's regard. 'The local police answered the 999 call within minutes. They wanted to know exactly where people were when Vyner killed himself. Maria told them about the phone call, what her husband and Vyner were doing. Vyner's last will is invalid. Loeb's submitting the old one for probate.'

The grey-haired policeman spun round as Page put his head back and laughed. Page wiped his eyes with his handkerchief.

'I love it,' he said. 'I just wish that the bastard had known.'

Drusilla laid her palm across her father's mouth. 'All that's over, Papa. You and I are starting again.'

Raven heaved himself up. 'I'm on my way. You people have a lot to talk about.'

Page gave Raven his hand. 'You'll be hearing from me,' he said, smiling.

Drusilla came closer. 'Will you promise to keep in touch?'

He shrugged. 'You're here. I'm here. I'll let you off lightly, I promise.'

She kissed him, this time, on both cheeks. 'Good bye, honorary godfather.'

'Good bye,' he said, head on one side, looking at her and then her father. 'And good bye to you.'

In many ways, Raven thought, he and Page were alike. Both were loose cannons.

He rode the lift down to the street and went past the waiting reporters. No one spoke to him. He chanced on a taxi at the next set of traffic-lights.

'Harrods,' he said to the driver.

The Floral Hall smelled of wet spring. The girl who came forward to serve him was pert and well-mannered. The pertness was in her eyes, the courtesy in her smile.

'Is there any way I can help you, sir?'

'Yes,' he said, looking round at the massed display of flowers. 'Can you arrange for some red roses to be delivered overseas?'

She leaned her weight on one heel, the rest of her body tilted towards him.

'Yes indeed, sir. Anywhere in the civilised world.'

He grinned. 'Does that include Canada?'

'Especially Canada,' she answered dead-pan.

'I want a dozen red roses sent to Kirstie Raven, 1108 Dundas Grove, York Mills, Metro-Toronto. Can I send a message?'

Her pen was still poised. 'Of course.'

'Just put "From Harry The Rat With Women",' he said; and paid for the flowers.

She was still smiling when he looked back on his way out. It warmed him against the cold on the street. With any sort of luck one day would continue to follow another and, in just two weeks' time, Kirstie would be home.